"I've never in my life been kissed like that."

He kept his eyes on her lovely face. Her expression appeared overwrought. He wanted to kiss her again. He hadn't found the extra strength to free her, but he knew he had to call a stop. "Would you want to change anything?" He brushed back a few springy tendrils from her temples.

Carol took time to find an answer. "You could break my heart, Damon. I'd forgive you."

Her answer rocked him. For the second time he had to pitch a fierce battle for control. Eventually his sense of what was best for them won out. He lifted her to her feet. "I would never do that."

"Not deliberately. *No.*" Carol placed her hands against his chest.

They had left their close and comfortable relationship way behind. That relationship had taken a giant leap into the unknown. Those ecstatic moments between them could not be taken back. Unforgettable as they were, it didn't guarantee ownership over the other or increasing intimacy between them. There were hazards ahead for both of them to overcome.

Welcome to the intensely emotional world of

USA TODAY bestselling author
Margaret Way

where rugged, brooding bachelors meet their match in the burning heart of Australia....

Praise for the author:

"Margaret Way delivers...vividly written, dramatic stories."
—*RT Book Reviews*

"With climactic scenes, dramatic imagery and bold characters, Margaret Way makes the Outback come alive."
—*RT Book Reviews*

Guardi

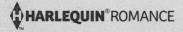

HARLEQUIN®ROMANCE

Recycling programs
for this product may
not exist in your area.

ISBN-13: 978-0-373-17863-6

GUARDIAN TO THE HEIRESS

First North American Publication 2013

Printed in U.S.A.

™ www.Harlequin.com

USA TODAY bestselling author **Margaret Way** was born and raised in the River City of Brisbane, capital of Queensland, Australia. A conservatorium trained professional musician, in 1969 she decided to fulfill a childhood dream to write a book and have it published. She submitted a manuscript to the iconic publishing firm of Mills & Boon (now Harlequin UK) in London. To her delight, the manuscript received immediate acceptance. The first book, *King Country,* published in 1970, was an outstanding success that heralded the start of a long and very successful career. The author hopes and believes the two goals she set herself since the beginning of her writing career have been achieved: first and foremost, to bring pleasure and relaxation to her global readership; second, to open up a window to the world on her own beautiful, unique country, captivating the hearts of her readers as they identify with rural and outback Australia and the Dreamtime culture of its Australian indigenous people. An award-winning author of more than 130 books, published in 114 countries in 34 languages, Margaret Way is a three-time finalist for a Romance Writers of Australia RUBY Award.

Recent books by Margaret Way

THE ENGLISH LORD'S SECRET SON
ARGENTINIAN IN THE OUTBACK*
THE CATTLE KING'S BRIDE*
MASTER OF THE OUTBACK
IN THE AUSTRALIAN BILLIONAIRE'S ARMS
HER OUTBACK COMMANDER
AUSTRALIA'S MAVERICK MILLIONAIRE

* The Langdon Dynasty duet

Other titles by this author available in ebook format.

This book is dedicated to my wonderful
Management Team

PROLOGUE

It wasn't the best of times for Selwyn Chancellor. Lying in his massive carved mahogany bed, he was moving in and out of consciousness, lost in a darkening sea of foreboding. Wave upon wave of memories tossed him about. Figures came and went. All the while his fragmented dreams were attended by excruciating pain that morphine was barely touching.

He was dying; he knew that. He welcomed death. It would come as a relief—*that* from a man who had lived his life refusing to face the fact one day he would die like everybody else. Only, he wasn't everyone else, was he? He was Selwyn Chancellor, billionaire several times over, a man of power and wide-reaching influence, rich beyond even his own dreams. He had lived and would die a rich man, president of the Chancellor Group, a conglomeration of trading companies, real-estate companies, manufacturing enterprises, transport services and insurance, with investments in many countries around the globe.

The father he had worshipped, Sir Edwin Chancellor, knighted by the Queen for his services to industry, had always urged him to excellence. His father at the end of his days had prophesised his brilliant future: *I know I can count on you, Selwyn, to build on my achievements. I leave the Chancellor Group in safe hands.*

His father, a legendary hard-nosed pragmatist, had been

proud of him. His father's approval had meant everything in the world to him; but none of that counted now. At the end of his extraordinary life he had been forced to concede the moments of true happiness in his life had been few and far between. He'd known some would genuinely mourn him just as he'd known the minute their family doctor, Harry Mc-Dowell, declared him dead "the Vultures" would move in.

"The Vultures" was his private name for his family. Not very nice, but justified. There was his son Maurice, by his deeply reserved wife, Elaine. His son's wife, Dallas, who had started out so attractive but had quickly gone to seed. At least Elaine had never done that, but Elaine had been unfitted by temperament to be the wife of an increasingly powerful man. To bring her lifestyle traumas to a head, had come the premature death of their beloved son Adam, their first born. Not all that long after, Elaine had ended her own life, though the coronial finding had labelled it an accident.

He knew better. He knew it *all*. Tragedy had clung to him. Maybe he had brought it on, however unwittingly.

It was Adam who was to have succeeded him; Adam who had all the necessary skills and strength of character to step into his shoes. Maurice, his younger son, had always lived in Adam's shadow, never effective enough in any of the family businesses, too indolent and too greedy to strike out on his own. The same could be said of Maurice's son—his playboy grandson Troy—who, of all of them, had taken the most pleasure in watching him die. Oh, the boy had covered it well, even feigning sorrow, but Selwyn could read his grandson like a book. Troy was and always would be hungry for money. Not that all three of them wouldn't have their hands out for their share. He knew there would be plenty of in-fighting. Blood was thinner than water when it came to money.

In a moment of blessed clarity he saw the stocky white-clad nurse move away from the window, checking her watch.

Time for another injection. The woman had an obsession with punctuality. He saw her place her tray on the bedside table then pick up a syringe, flicking it to expel air, preparatory to injecting the powerful drug into his near-useless arm. She was about to jab him when he summoned up all his remaining strength, startling her so badly she let out a shriek. A fruit bat couldn't have done it any better.

"Leave it, woman. Leave me be. Go away."

Her mouth opened and closed like a beached fish, but whatever she wanted to say she thought better of it. No words emerged. He supposed, with bitter humour, she could understand his family's wishing to be rid of the old tyrant. She wasn't such a fool that she wouldn't have cottoned on to the fact his family was a seething cauldron of emotions. Over the past week of his serious decline he had witnessed those emotions coming to a rolling boil. One of them could even take it into their head to finish him off; an overdose of a powerful drug would be especially tempting. A soft pillow held down just long enough?

"Well, then, what are you waiting for?" he rasped.

"Doctor McDowell will be here around two." She spoke in a reproachful way.

"Is that supposed to make me feel better?"

A flash of hostility came into her eyes. "You'll be requiring another injection well before that, sir."

"Don't get lippy with me, woman. Get out of here. If you allow any member of my family into this room, it means instant dismissal."

A sweat had broken out on the nurse's forehead. She was extremely well-paid, well-housed and well-fed. No one had wanted to look after the old man. "Is there anything I can do before I go?"

"Wh-a-t?" Selwyn Chancellor had all but forgotten her. "No. Just go."

The nurse went, wearing an aggrieved face.

Alone, all alone, on a storm-tossed sea.

One was always alone when dying. He could hear his own laboured breathing. Maybe death was freedom? Nice to think so. Maybe he would meet up again with the people he had loved and lost. Maybe they would *come* for him? The thought made him smile. And as he smiled he was granted one last vision…

"These are for you, Poppy." A beautiful little girl, five years old with a crown of ruby-red curls, put a posy of spring flowers into his hand.

"They're lovely, sweetheart!" he exclaimed, burying his nose in the fragrant offering, knowing he was risking a barrage of sneezes. "Thank you so much."

"I love you, Poppy," she told him, dancing around happily. Carol was never still. Little Carol, the only person in the world to love him unreservedly.

"I love you, too, my darling," he said with perfect sincerity. He was seated out on the rear terrace, finishing off a last cup of coffee before setting off for the city. Time to go. He stood up, a tall, vigorous man, taking her soft little hand.

"What are you going to do today?" he asked. It was a Saturday. He knew her mother, Roxanne, wouldn't bother taking her anywhere. The proverbial cat was a better mother than Roxanne, but he had employed an excellent nanny, a highly qualified, pleasant, middle-aged woman, experienced with looking after children. She and Carol got on famously.

"Can't you and Daddy stay home and be with me, Poppy?" she implored.

"Not possible, sweetheart," he said, brushing a hand over her springy curls. "Your father and I have business to attend to. Important business."

"Can't it wait?" She was impatient.

"Afraid not," he said, casting around for something to appease her. "What about tomorrow? We could take a run out to Beaumont. How would that suit you?" He would have to make the time and effort, but his granddaughter was worth it.

She clapped her hands, looking up at him with sparkling cerulean-blue eyes. "That would be wonderful. You're the best poppy in the whole wide world," she announced, picking up his large hand and kissing it...

He couldn't suppress a sob. Tears stung his eyes. It hadn't been all that much longer before his little sweetheart had disappeared from his life along with his son Adam. His emotions had changed rapidly, savagely, from a reasonable contentment to a grief-stricken hatred. But he had kept his eye on his granddaughter, albeit from afar. Powerful as he then was, a *mother* had proved to be more powerful. But he had seen to it his little Carol was well provided for. The treacherous Roxanne had remarried a City identity, Jeff Emmett, a scant eighteen months after Adam's death, but she had gone on sending him all the bills pertaining to Carol's upkeep. Greed. As Adam's widow, she had benefited greatly. He had paid up unquestioningly. Hadn't he built up scrapbook after scrapbook of Carol's young life and achievements over the years? He had watched her from a distance, locked away in the back seat of his Rolls. He'd had his best, most discreet private investigator keep an eye on her, her mother and stepfather.

A year before, when he had found out he had cancer—and not gall trouble, as he had supposed—he had called in a solicitor. Not steady-as-she-goes Marcus Bradfield, senior partner of Bradfield Douglass, but the new young fellow—the associate, Damon Hunter—the one who had come up with all the fresh ideas to save his companies' money. It was Hunter who had drawn up his new will. Selwyn had urged him to get shot of Bradfield Douglass and go out on his own, though he was sure in time the young man would be offered a full partnership. It could be no more than his due.

He'd had plenty of experience picking the ones who would go to the top. Nevertheless he'd had Hunter thoroughly investigated. He had come up trumps in all departments. Hunter was chosen to guard Carol's money and her interests until she turned twenty-one the following August. God knew, Hunter was young himself, but he had been when he'd started to make his mark. Hunter was his man.

Carol was family more than anyone else. Carol was Adam's daughter, Adam's only child. Adam had planned on more children, only life had cheated all three of them—most of all his sad, sweet Elaine. It was his turn now to cheat the gathering Vultures.

In his very last moments, Selwyn Chancellor was rewarded with another vision of his granddaughter, the last time he had seen her. Had she looked across the busy city street, she would have spotted the luxury car but she had been too busy chatting to one of her girlfriends, a fellow university student he had seen her with several times. She looked so beautiful, so vital, and beyond that so happy, a sense of peace had settled on him. He had always blamed himself—at least in part—for the way things had turned out, but now he felt a burden was lifted from his shoulders. He trusted Damon Hunter to look after Carol's best interests and he wasn't a man given to trust.

He had to be hallucinating—his poor head was so sick and muddled—but he fancied he saw his little Elaine come to stand at the end of his bed. His immediate reaction was to hold out his hand.

"Is that you, Elaine?" he whispered, straining upwards.

She didn't speak, but she drew nearer, like the spirit appointed to take care of his soul.

His vision grew clearer. It *was* Elaine. She was *shining,* a silver haze surrounding her. He wasn't afraid; he was eager to join her.

Selwyn Chancellor reached out to take his wife's hand.

A farewell to arms.

CHAPTER ONE

DAMON HUNTER WAS placing some files into his briefcase when Marcus Bradfield walked through the open door of his office, an attempt at a solemn expression on his handsome, fleshy face. Oddly enough, the extra padding in his cheeks lent him the air of a middle-aged cherub. "Bit of news."

Damon broke off what he was doing, directly meeting his boss's gaze. "Don't tell me—Selwyn Chancellor's dead."

"Exactly right." Bradfield sank heavily into one of the armchairs in front of Damon's desk. Bradfield was an affluent man, born of wealth, well-respected, a leading light of the city's elite. His grandfather, Patrick Bradfield, had been one of the original partners who had founded Bradfield Douglass. "Maurice rang me." A faint smile spread across Bradfield's face. "He did his best, but he didn't sound all that grief-stricken."

"Difficult when you're glad," Damon commented briefly. He had no time for Maurice Chancellor. Ditto for Champagne Charlie, the son Troy. "Why didn't he ring me, as well? I'm handling the will."

"Maurice likes to deal with the *top* people, Damon," Bradfield said with a smirk. "Selwyn Chancellor has employed this firm for many long years. I'm a full partner. You're still an associate. Am I right?"

"And I'm quite sure there will be a full partnership on

offer in the near future," Damon countered, knowing it to be true. He had brought a lot of new business to the firm. In fact, he was gaining a reputation in the City as the can-do guy. "I still say he should have rung me, after he rang you." He held firm. "That was the correct thing to do."

"Poor man was in shock." Bradfield gave way to a wry chuckle. "I said I'd tell you."

"Not good enough! Did he tell you he'd contacted Carol Emmett, his niece? The family may have been estranged for years, but clearly she must be told."

"Didn't mention young Carol." Bradfield waved that one away. "Why would he? He hasn't acknowledged her since the big rift. Now there's a beautiful girl. Met her a number of times. She darn nearly charmed the pants off me."

"You wish."

"Okay, so I'm getting on, as my dear wife never fails to remind me. Bit wild, young Carol, I hear."

"Just *young,*" Damon clipped off, thinking Carol Emmett not only looked a handful she was bound to be one. "She has to know."

"I dare say the old man remembered her?" Bradfield gave Damon one of his guileless stares.

"He did that." Damon kept his face neutral. "She was his granddaughter."

"He paid her no attention at all!" Condemnation was in Bradfield's blue eyes. Marcus was a staunch family man with three daughters of marriageable age.

"As far as you know."

Marcus gave him a long, searching look. "Damon, you know as well as I do, the family as good as abandoned her and her mother. Now, there's a swinger, that Roxanne! A real glamour girl, though no one seems to like her. You should hear my wife! Another thing, my boy—"

"I'm not your boy, Marcus."

"Another thing, *my man,* Maurice wants this kept quiet until morning when the press will be informed. Selwyn Chancellor was an important man. The premier could even want a state funeral."

"Against Selwyn Chancellor's wishes?" Damon shook his head. "He stipulated a quiet funeral, family and a few chosen friends only. He is to be buried in the garden of his country home, Beaumont, where I assume he died. Carol is to be invited."

"Not Jeff and Roxanne?" Bradfield asked as though that violated some set of rules.

"No way. Jeff Emmett might be one of your 'good ole boys,' but he and Roxanne are specifically excluded."

"So bygones won't be bygones? We all know Selwyn and his wife—what was her name again?"

"Elaine," Damon supplied.

"Blamed Roxanne for the death of their son Adam, the heir apparent. It was a bit suspicious you have to admit—all set to go through the Heads for a good day's sailing, only Adam takes a wallop on the head from the boom on the mainsail before pitching into the harbour. Roxanne tries to chuck in a lifebuoy, finds it unfastened but still attached, so she throws in every cushion to hand, anything that would float. Meanwhile the boat is moving on at around eight knots."

"She couldn't swim. That much was true."

"I've always said, men don't teach their wives enough about boats and light aircraft. They rely on always being there."

"I agree. Roxanne was believed."

"Not by everybody." Bradfield sighed. "Even to mention the case to my darling wife is to get into a heated argument. Old Selwyn didn't believe her; the mother was the more vehement of the two. She never accepted the coroner's finding. We're both yachtsmen so we know what can happen. But

Adam Chancellor's parents continued to hold their daughter-in-law guilty of some crime."

"Maybe she was," Damon suggested. "She certainly acted strangely in the days that followed—not a sign of a tear, always dressed up to the nines. Not that that makes her guilty of anything. But the whole thing was a bit strange; I've read up on it all. The tragedy damn near split the city in two. But, whatever story Roxanne Chancellor told, it worked. As far as I'm concerned, more questions were asked than there were answers for."

Bradfield stared down at his locked hands, as though they might hold the answer. "Speculation won't get us anywhere. It was years ago. Just about everyone has forgotten."

"Not true, Marcus."

"Why so judgemental?" Bradfield asked, not wanting to take the issue further. "The verdict is what counts. Jeff Emmett did the right thing—he adopted Roxanne's little daughter not long after they were married."

"I'm sure Roxanne forced him into it. No love lost between her and the Chancellor family." Damon gathered up his briefcase. "Look, I'm out of here. It's been a long day." For some time now he had been the first to arrive and often the last to leave.

Marcus cranked to his feet. He had put on a good deal of weight in the past few years, with his tailor gamely keeping pace. "Me, too. They mightn't have slung Roxanne into jail, as some in the family no doubt wanted, but she copped plenty of torture. You'll want to tell your client as soon as possible."

Damon started to the door. "I intend to."

Bradfield stayed him with a hand on his shoulder. "You're coming Saturday night?"

"Wouldn't miss it." Damon managed to sound enthusiastic when he didn't really want to go to Julie Bradfield's just-the-right-side-of-thirty birthday party.

"Every night I go down on my knees and pray my Julie finds a good husband," Marcus confided. One prayer stuck in the groove; Damon knew Marcus had his eye on him.

"And I'm sure she'll find one." Damon gave his boss a reassuring smile.

As long as it's not me.

He knew her address; one of the inner suburbs. She had moved out of the Emmett house as soon as she'd started university. He knew she was studying law, a good student who could do so much better if she put her mind to it. He had his sources at the university where he had graduated top of his class. Carol Emmett wasn't known as a party girl precisely, but the word was she was "wildly popular." She was certainly social. There was hardly a venue she visited where she wasn't photographed by what passed for the paparazzi. He knew her by her press coverage. She was ravishingly pretty, if pint-sized, with a mop of lustrous red curls, porcelain skin and brilliant blue eyes.

It was his job to find her and as soon as possible.

The unit Carol Emmett and two of her girlfriends were renting was part of a block of twenty. Most of the units were rented out to the better-heeled university students who knew they had to stick to certain rules or they'd be out the door. The block was in a good, mainly residential area with a small park nearby. There was security; that was good. He went up to the door and was about to press the button for apartment eight when two young women emerged from the lift. Their outfits—one of them was wearing a mega-short skirt exposing more than just her plump knees—indicated they were having a night out on the town. They gave him a giggling, comprehensive once-over. They would definitely know him again. He was a guy who stood out, not only for his height— six-two—his chiselled good looks, but his aura of success.

"Who are you looking for, handsome?" The cheekier of the two, the one with the plump knees, spoke, a bright, inquisitive expression on her face.

"Carol Emmett." He answered in a relaxed way, but it came out with in-built authority.

"Well, you can't be the cops!" Cheeky eyed his beautifully tailored Italian business-suit, the shirt, the tie, even the shoes on his feet.

"Certainly not. I come as a friend."

"Ooh, lucky Caro!" she whistled, continuing to study him, her head tipped to one side. "Bit old for her, though, aren't you? Like, the guys Caro dates are *our* age."

Was thirty old these days? How depressing. "So you do know her?"

"Course we do," the other girl chimed in. She was plain, with an extraordinary hot-pink streak in her dark spiked hairdo, no doubt to shift focus from an over-long nose. "She's our flatmate. You won't find her at home. She's out looking for Trace."

"And Trace would be?"

"One of our mates," the cheeky one supplied, still eyeing him over. "Trace is always getting herself into trouble. Caro likes to keep an eye on her."

"Any idea where she might have headed? I need to discuss a business matter with her. It's urgent."

The two girls looked at each other, before deciding on giving him the information he sought. Evidently he had passed muster. "I'd say Trace's little hidey-hole," Cheeky said. "She doesn't live here; can't afford it. We can't either, only for Caro. She helps us out. She's not in any trouble, is she?" Both girls suddenly looked concerned.

"Of course not. I only need to speak to her. Where does Trace—I assume that's Tracey—live?"

Cheeky supplied the address which was in a less salubrious inner-city suburb. He knew he could find it easily.

A narrow winding street snaked between too many overhanging trees. He didn't like the idea of a young girl walking down this street at night. He would make a call the next morning to see if he could get those trees loped. He parked behind a car with a personalised number-plate that as good as announced Carol Emmett was inside. She was exactly where her flatmates had said she would be, checking on Trace; he didn't like it. Whether her name had changed to Emmett or not, everyone knew she was Selwyn Chancellor's granddaughter, albeit estranged. It was her grandfather's dying wish she revert to her father's name. From now on Carol Chancellor would need a bodyguard. Such a man would have to be unobtrusive, very probably with his function kept from his charge.

He exited his car and locked it, looking up at an old Victorian house that had been converted into flats. It would have been an impressive house in its day. It still was, despite the current owner's neglect. There was no security. That didn't surprise him. The front door was even ajar. He pushed it gently, walking into the hallway before scanning the names of the tenants listed on the wall. Not that he needed to. The girls had told him that Trace lived with her boyfriend in flat number six. The tone had indicated they didn't approve of Trace's boyfriend, who wasn't a university student. "Calls himself a chef," Cheeky had supplied with a snort. "Works in a sandwich bar."

"He was a chef, Amanda. Got kicked out. Temper, remember?"

He was halfway up the stairs when he heard shouting. The language was far from polite. He took the rest of the stairs at a rush. A raised male voice drowned out a young woman's. The accent was educated, though she wasn't averse to the odd swear word or two. She didn't sound afraid, rather she sounded angry, challenging. With the wrong man that tone of voice was courting trouble. He had real reason to be concerned. He didn't think that voice belonged to Tracey. It belonged to Carol Emmett, soon to be Chancellor again.

He moved silently to the door and gave it a thump with his fist. The scruffy young man that came to the door was maybe twenty-five or-six, handsome, not tall but heavily muscled. He was wearing a tight T-shirt, no doubt to show off his physique. He looked strong. But depressingly stupid.

"What d'ya want?"

"Well, that's to the point, if nothing else." The show of aggression did nothing for Damon. "I'd like a word with Ms Emmett, if I may? She's inside, isn't she?"

"Why would she wanna talk to you? Slumming, are yah?" The veins on the young man's neck were standing out.

"Can I have *your* name?" Damon asked crisply.

That confused the guy. "Yah gotta be joking."

"Not at all." Damon stared him down. "Step away from the door, please. I want to see Ms Emmett and her friend, Tracey. Do I take it you're the boyfriend?"

The young man fired up. "Get outta here. You're not the cops." He went to slam the door, only Damon shoved him out of the way and drove the door forward. At the same time he sighted a young dark-haired woman slumped in a chair. The cheekbone nearest him was heavily bruised, the eye almost closed. That upset him; he had seen too many incidences of abuse of women by their partners. The worst part was the victims often backed up for more. The damage was as much psychological as physical. Some women actually believed they had been asking for punishment.

Another young woman, who had to be Carol Emmett, was hurrying from the direction of the kitchen, clutching an ice-pack like a weapon. His immediate impression was she was infinitely lovelier in the flesh. He took in the tousled mane of ruby hair, her glowing skin—he had never seen skin glow like that—and her beautiful eyes of an intense sparkling blue. She was dressed in a short silk tunic, turquoise with a broad band of amethyst at the hem. It showed off her slender legs to perfection. There wasn't a hint of a generous curve. She was built like a ballerina. She even had a ballerina's trick of appearing to be in motion when she wasn't.

"What's going on here?" she demanded in that clear voice that gave notice she would soon find out. So, an imperious bantam weight! She could only be five-three at most. "Who are you?" She gave Damon a sharp, questioning look.

He darn near laughed, only the boyfriend took advantage of the distraction. He made a fist around the set of keys he quickly yanked out of the door, and then came at Damon in a bullocking rush, swearing and snarling.

Two things happened at once. Carol Emmett, blue eyes blazing, hurled the icepack like a missile at the boyfriend's head. It missed, but only because Damon, using his height and speed advantage, had his assailant in a deftly imposed arm-lock. The violent boyfriend was on his knees, his left arm twisted high behind his back, his right arm anchored to the floor with Damon's shoe pressed down hard on his hand.

"You're dead, mate." The boyfriend made the threat, straining unsuccessfully to free himself.

"Gosh, I won't sleep at night." Damon got a grip on the guy's shirt collar before heaving him up into a chair which the enterprising Ms Emmett pushed into position.

"This is called instant bonding." She met his eyes, her lovely mouth upturned in a smile.

"You're shaping up as a pretty good offsider. I'm your new solicitor, by the way. I'm quite prepared to act for Tracey. This is the guy who assaulted her?"

A denial came on a burst of genuine outrage. "Come on! I just smacked her around a little. She likes it."

Tracey didn't say anything, but Carol Emmett exploded. "It's a good thing I got here when I did." She looked directly at Damon, her face filled with disgust. "God knows what might have happened. This isn't the first time, is it, Tarik?" she said with searing contempt.

"You're no pal of Tracey's," he yelled over his shoulder, clenching every muscle. "This is all your fault! Why don't you mind your own business? I'll get square. Don't you worry about that."

Angered by the threat, Damon exerted ever-increasing pressure.

"You'll break my bloody arm, mate." Tarik, the abuser, was full of self-pity.

"It is possible," Damon said, the voice of dispassion, knowing the point to stop. "Call the police, Carol." He looked to her, not absolutely sure she wasn't planning to hit the boyfriend with the glass paperweight near to hand.

"No, no!" Tracey finally found her voice. The note in her voice sent a shiver down Damon's spine. Hadn't he heard that note before?

Carol rounded on her friend, looking dismayed. "What's wrong with you, Trace? Can't you see what this guy's capable of?"

"Why don't you sit down, Ms Emmett?" Damon advised, trying to steer the situation into calmer waters. "Let *me* ask the questions."

She raised her brows. "Go right head," she said dryly. "You're my new solicitor, right? News to me. I don't have a solicitor."

The boyfriend let out a sneering laugh. "Caught out, eh?"

"Bradfield Douglass." Damon found his business card, handing it to Carol Emmett. "Damon Hunter at your service.

And this young lady's, too. She obviously needs help." Tracey had straightened up, so now Damon could see the full extent of her injuries. They extended to around her neck.

"Good God!" he breathed in dismay. "Do what I say, Carol. Call the police."

"Right away." She sped away to the landline, without glancing back at her friend, who didn't speak again.

While Carol Emmett made the call, the boyfriend seized a last opportunity to get away. He got to his feet again, shaping up and looking dangerous. Only Damon was taller, stronger, in excellent shape. He worked out regularly at a boxing gym. He found the exercise both tough and relaxing after long hours at his desk. The owner, an ex-middleweight champion who could still box the ears off anyone, had become not only his sparring partner but friend.

For his pains, the boyfriend was yanked back in his chair, looking as though he'd been hit by a train.

Tracey witnessed the whole thing. "Thank God!" She breathed a heartfelt sigh, her voice hoarse from the injury to her throat. "I've been such a fool."

"Don't I know it!" said Carol, not about to make soothing noises. "But don't worry, Trace. We'll get you through this. I'll throw a few things in a bag, and then I'm going to take you back to our place. You can't stay here any more." She looked across at Damon. "She can take out an AVO against him, right? He must be kept away from her."

He nodded. "I'll have it seen to." They all turned their heads at the sound of the heavy boots on the stairs.

"That'll be the police now," Carol announced, relief mixed with satisfaction.

Tarik scowled. "I'm gonna complain you assaulted me." He fixed Damon with a look of loathing.

Damon gave a brief laugh. "Go for it!"

"I've got witnesses."

A hoot from Carol. "Shut up, Tarik. Tracey is the one with the witness to your attack."

"You won't stop me," he threatened, trying to catch his girlfriend's eye. He had found it easy enough to control her. He had the knack.

"We'll see about that." Damon's tone was curt. He knew men of Tarik's type couldn't be counted on to obey the law. In fact, they were proud of flouting it.

"Police," a tough male voice boomed from the front door.

There was a big smile on Carol Emmett's face. "I have to say, that was quick!"

"What, did you offer a reward?" Tarik sneered.

"I was on the point of it," she replied, going swiftly to the door.

In the end, after initial statements had been given, Damon followed Carol's little silver car to her flat. Tracey was tucked into the back seat, nursing her injuries, although she had refused point blank to go to the hospital to have herself checked out.

"I'm okay!" It was almost as if she feared presenting herself at Accident and Emergency.

"How do you know?" Carol had shot back.

"I know." For once Tracey was adamant.

End of argument.

It was almost an hour later before Carol had settled her friend. After a shower, clean nightwear and pain killers, Tracey allowed herself to be tucked into Carol's bed. Carol had assured her friend it would be no problem for her to sleep on the three-seater sofa in the living room.

"I've done it before."

She hadn't, although all manner of their friends had.

When she finally returned to the living room, she found

Damon inspecting a group of photographs she'd put into a large frame and hung on a wall.

Damon had been expecting the usual student clutter, but what he had seen of the three-bedroom apartment—open-plan kitchen and living room—was a neat, very attractive dwelling place that had been furnished in a stylish way. He liked the three-piece lounge suite in genuine cream leather. There was a glass-topped circular table with four yellow cushioned rattan chairs arranged around it for dining. A wooden bookcase packed with a wide range of books, from romances to far more weighty tomes, stood in a corner. A large abstract painting hung over a Chinese altar table. A distance away to either side of the altar table stood a pair of traditional Chinese cabinets with horizontal open-work panels. Yellow curtains hung at the plate-glass doors that gave onto a small balcony where four yellow glazed pots planted with strelitzias were lined up against the balustrade.

"You're taking an interest." There was a faint taunt in her voice.

"Just admiring the decor. Someone has created a certain style. I love the Chinese pieces." He bent to take a closer look at the cabinets. He thought the wood was *huanghuali,* the principal hardwood used by Chinese cabinet makers. He thought he was right dating them as late Qing.

"Me, too," she said, offhandedly. "As for the decorating, someone had to make the effort. And find the money."

"I'm sure your friends appreciate it."

"Well…" She let a further comment slide. She knew her flatmates took advantage of her. She allowed it. "Like a cup of coffee? Glass of wine? Maybe a salad? You could join me. I haven't had a thing to eat."

It suddenly struck him he was hungry. "That'd be nice, Carol. May I call you Carol?"

"Caro," she said. She made a point of being called Caro.

"Carol is such a beautiful name."

"What do you want from me, Damon?" She moved behind the black granite kitchen counter. "Is there something you have to tell me? Something about the family?"

She didn't look in the least perturbed, so he decided to give it to her straight. From what he'd seen of her, he thought she could handle it. "Your grandfather passed away late this afternoon, Carol—at Beaumont, his country estate."

Her blue eyes, a wonderful contrast to her ruby-red hair, flew to his across the dividing space. "You're absolutely sure about that?"

"Yes," he replied.

"So it's all over," she said, turning to pull out plates.

"Not for you, Carol," he pointed out with some gravity. "You're a major beneficiary in his will."

She swung back sharply, her porcelain cheeks flushed over her high cheekbones. "You've got to be joking!"

"In no way. I'm your appointed lawyer."

She stared at him. He was no more than thirty, she estimated, though his manner had a self-assurance far beyond those years. He projected high intelligence and a quite staggering sexuality. He had everything going for him, the entire package: tall, dark and handsome; his classic features not bland but distinctive. He had a great head of hair, coal-black with a natural wave, brilliant dark eyes that took in everything at a glance.

She had the oddest feeling of recognition. Had she seen him before? She couldn't have. She would have remembered; maybe a photograph in a glossy magazine, squiring some glamour girl? He looked just the kind of guy who attracted women in droves. The name, too, seemed familiar. *Damon Hunter. Damon Hunter.* It came to her in flash—Professor Deakin's star pupil. The most outstanding student of law Professor Deakin had ever had the pleasure of teaching. That was pretty cool.

She appeared so engrossed in her speculations, Damon had to prompt her. "I hope I pass muster?" His resonant voice carried humour.

"You look like you make tons of money," was her terse response. She had read about instant high-level arousal in novels. She hadn't encountered it—until now. He was arousing feelings of which she had scarcely been aware. Not that he'd be interested in her. She was a twenty-year-old student, not some voluptuous beauty with a goodly share of experience in bed.

"Is that important?" he asked.

She had a sudden picture of herself as an instrument; a man like him could play a woman's feelings at will. She shook her head so vigorously, her curls bounced. "No, but I thought Marcus Bradfield was my grandfather's solicitor."

"Was for many years," he said. "But your grandfather appointed me in this case. I wanted to tell you about his death before anyone else did, or you simply saw it on TV. The media will have the news by now."

"The great man is dead. Long live the king," she said rather mournfully. "I shudder to think it might be Uncle Maurice?"

"We have to wait to see what transpires. Mind if I take off my jacket?"

"Go right ahead." As she guessed he had a great body; all of his movements had an athlete's grace. So, lawyer and action man. He had taken Tarik, who was strong, down without raising a sweat. She watched him place his tailored jacket over a chair before he loosened his silk tie. His every movement was imprinting itself on her brain. This was ridiculous. So ridiculous, she resented it.

She took the makings of a salad out of the crisper. "I don't need a penny of his money. The way he treated me, the way the family treated me, was monstrous."

He heard the deep hurt beneath the condemnation in her voice. "I agree, but I didn't come here with apologies, Carol. The will speaks for itself. Your grandfather clearly wanted to make reparation."

"My grandfather with the stone heart! Does the rest of the family know? My Uncle Maurice, Dallas and my creepy cousin Troy—I see him around. He's even tried to chat me up. What a joke!"

"Has he really?" Damon found himself not liking that one bit. Her tone had implied Troy Chancellor's approach hadn't been cousinly.

"Alas, yes. I don't like him. Let's eat, before you tell me any more. I'm fast losing my appetite."

"Can I help?"

She shook her head. "A salad is simplicity itself. Let me get you a glass of wine—red or white?"

"I'll have red, if you've got it?"

"Mmm, I think so. Have a look in there." She pointed to one of the Chinese cabinets.

He didn't open the beaded doors immediately. He stood studying the piece of furniture that stood on rounded straight feet. "You know what you've got here?"

"I do indeed." Her tone mocked. "I have a pair of pagoda-form side tables in my bedroom, but you're not going in there."

"You like Oriental furniture?" That was obvious. He knew Selwyn Chancellor had been a major collector.

"Who wouldn't? If I get to know you well enough, I'll show you my celadon jade carving. *Qianlong*."

"Ah, another collector in the making."

"I'm told I have the eye."

"I'm sure you have. Like your grandfather. He was a re-

nowned collector." He opened one of the cabinet doors, studying the labels before selecting a bottle of Tasmanian pinot
noir.

"I know." Suddenly she was remembering the endless
treasure trove her grandfather and his father before him had
collected over the years. She had been just a little girl, yet
her memories had stayed with her—the way her grandfather had held her hand as he had walked her down the long
gallery filled with pictures in gilded frames, telling her the
names of the artists and a little about them. She remembered
his jade collection in the tall glass cabinets; all the Chinese
porcelains; the tall "soldier" vases enamelled with birds and
flowers; the blue and white porcelain; the *famille rose* and
the *famille noir.* She remembered the wonderful *famille verte*
fishbowls on their rosewood stands that had stood in the hallway. They'd always been filled with big pots of cymbidium
orchids in full bloom. And this Damon Hunter asked her if
she knew what she had?

He was saying something to her, but she could scarcely
hear him. She was afraid she would burst into tears, she who
never cried. How could a grandfather who had loved her so
much turn heartless? She remembered how her mother had
hated him and had inexplicably hated her gentle grandmother,
who was so quiet and retiring and had always kept out of her
mother's way.

"Are you all right?"

She blinked hard, incensed she had come so close to weeping. "Of course I am," she said crossly. "What have you got
there?" Why wouldn't he spot her momentary upset? She
couldn't remember when she had seen such X-ray eyes.

"A Tasmanian pinot noir." He turned the bottle to show
her the label. "It's very good. Are you going to join me in a
glass, or don't you drink?"

"You know better," she said briefly. A few times too many

she had been photographed coming out of a nightclub with a few of her friends, looking a little on the wild side in short sparkly outfits with her hair in a mad crinkly halo. Okay so she enjoyed a glass of wine! She didn't touch drugs even when a few in her circle did. Soft drugs, the so called recreational kind. Getting high on drugs was of as much interest to her as bungee jumping.

He came behind the counter, so tall she thought she would just about reach his heart. He was a sexy piece of work and no mistake. She drew a deep breath, opening a drawer finding the bottle opener, then passing it to him. Their fingers touched.

Contact almost took her breath away. She grabbed a tea towel, as if to wipe the effect of it away. "The glasses are in the cupboard directly behind you," she said shortly, finishing off her green salad; fresh baby spinach leaves and peppery watercress with a chopped shallot, a quick dressing of extra virgin olive oil, balsamic vinegar with a little Dijon mustard then a grind of salt and black pepper. She had added some goat's cheese to the mix. Usually cubed croutons as well, but she didn't have the time. The succulent slices of ham were already sliced and on the white plates.

"That looks good," he said and meant it.

He was so close her body was humming like live power lines. "Super simple. You just have to make sure everything is fresh. My flatmates would live on takeaways if I weren't there. Takeaways aren't my scene."

"Not when one can whip up a delicious meal in ten or fifteen minutes."

She was at war with herself. She wanted him to move away. At the same time she wanted him to stay. She could smell his very subtle, very pleasant cologne. "So what do you survive on, or is there a woman in your life?" she asked briskly.

Bound to be.

"Simple food, Carol, but good, fresh produce," he answered, pouring the wine. "I don't do takeaways, either."

"Which doesn't answer the question."

"No permanent woman in my life, if that's what you mean."

She was pierced by some sensation she thought had to be embarrassment. "I thought I told you it was Caro."

"Maybe I got used to hearing your grandfather referring to you as Carol," he replied gently.

He appeared to enjoy the meal she had prepared. She couldn't taste a thing. To make up for it she had a second glass of wine. She realised what she was doing; she was trying to cover up an emotional crisis. Her collapse would have to wait for later. She had learned to keep her emotions to herself. Her mother wasn't the caring kind. Indeed, Roxanne had acted as though rearing a child, especially a daughter with a mind of her own, was a real penance. Her stepfather, Jeff, had been nice enough to her, but he had started getting too touchy around the time she'd turned sixteen. She had been glad to get out of the house; her mother was equally glad to see her go. Her mother had come to regard her as some sort of rival.

It didn't bear thinking about. She had no one really to confide in among her friends. They didn't know what it felt like to be Selwyn Chancellor's granddaughter, to be photographed wherever you went. They thought it was fun to be in the picture; she hated it. The invasion of privacy, it was a kind of violation.

"What are you thinking about?" Damon asked. He had been watching her face. She had such a range of expressions. He knew the absence of tears beyond that glitter didn't mean she wasn't suffering in her way. He had learned a lot about her mother and her stepfather—nothing much *good.*

He didn't want to think about what had made her break away. She was exquisitely pretty, like a Dresden figurine. He had heard it said her mother was as "hard as nails and twice as sharp." Apparently she couldn't deal with a daughter who, as she'd grown up, started to eclipse her. Now, that was sad—a kind of "mirror, mirror, on the wall" scenario. He wondered where Carol Emmett found comfort. Not that there would be any shortage of comforters. More now that she would have to cope with being the Chancellor heiress. The fortune hunters would emerge from the woodwork.

Afterwards he helped her clear the table. Carol made coffee. Her moment of weakness had passed. "So, what is it I'm required to do?"

"By tomorrow this will be front-page news, Carol. A media event. Your grandfather died at his country estate. That is where he wished to be buried."

"I know. In the garden at Beaumont, alongside my grandmother, Elaine. We used to go for walks there. The grounds were so beautiful, and so big I thought it was an enchanted forest and I was the princess. When I was about four, my grandfather told me where he wanted to be buried. He loved me, you know. *Then*." She swallowed hard.

"He always loved you, Carol," he felt compelled to say. He hadn't missed that little pained swallow. "He told me he'd wanted to fight your mother for custody."

She broke in fierily, flatly contradicting. "He did *not!*"

"Let me correct you—he did. As his legal advisors, we told him winning custody of you was one fight he wouldn't win. Your mother was your mother, a powerful person in your life. She was determined to keep you. She wasn't letting go."

"Spite, probably," Carol found herself saying. It shocked her because it very likely was true. She'd no idea up until that point her grandfather had wanted custody of her. She fully intended to take that up with her mother. "My mother hated the family—my uncle Maurice, his wife, Dallas, but particularly my grandfather. It took me years to find out he had practically accused her of murdering my father. She would *never* have done that. What would be the reason?" She spread her hands.

"Your grandparents didn't have a case."

"I know that." She didn't believe for a minute her mother had wanted to dispose of her father. But then her mother was so good at deception. In her mid-forties, Roxanne was still a beautiful, sexy woman, a born temptress. But she wasn't all that smart. Murder would have been difficult to pull off on the harbour. The Manly ferry, in fact, had come to her mother's rescue. Even the floating cushions had been retrieved; never her father's body. As a child she had prayed and prayed he had swum all the way to New Guinea, perhaps; he had never drowned, anything but that. Her father had been out on the harbour a million times. He was a fine sailor.

Damon Hunter's voice snapped her out of her unhappy thoughts. "Allow me to be the first to congratulate you, Carol. You're the Chancellor heiress."

She gave a bleak laugh. "So I might as well get back my father's name. I've never liked Emmett but it was a shield for the time. This won't make anyone in the family happy. I do hope they've all been well-provided for, or am I in for a lengthy court battle?"

"No battle. Your grandfather knew exactly what he was doing. Sound mind, sound intent. I drew up the will. It's iron-clad. I should tell you at this point I have control over your inheritance until you turn twenty-one, which I understand is August eighth, next year?"

She gave him a taunting smile. "That means you have charge of the purse strings?"

"We can always discuss what you need. You don't have to worry about any heavy-handed treatment. I'm here to protect your interests, Carol." *And to protect you,* he thought, jolted by his instantaneous attraction to her. It was like being handed a bouquet of the most beautiful red roses, perfect buds awaiting full bloom but spreading their fragrance. He couldn't think of a single young woman of his acquaintance who'd had that extraordinary effect on him.

"Sounds like I might need it," she said wryly. "The truth is, I don't want the money. On the other hand, I think I can do a lot of good. Rich people have a responsibility to give back to the community."

"Your grandfather certainly did that."

She couldn't deny it. "So here I am, an heiress without warning. I think I'm in shock."

"Well, you're not jumping up and down," he said.

There was such an attractive quirk to his handsome mouth. It struck her that her feelings were a bit extreme. "Everyone will hate me," she said. "Why would I feel elated? Except I am, in an odd way. It's not the money. It's the fact Poppy—my grandfather," she quickly corrected, "wanted custody of me. If only I'd known that. It would have given me some comfort."

She didn't say her own mother had denied her that comfort. In death, her grandfather had left her rich enough to be independent of everyone—first up, her mother. They didn't enjoy a good relationship. At least her mother had always been surprisingly generous when it came to providing for her. She had even bought her a flashy sports car when she had needed a car to get to and from university.

"You haven't asked how much." Damon wondered if she had any idea.

She shrugged a delicately boned shoulder. "I don't want to know. Not yet, anyway. That's way too mercenary. How much does anyone need? I just love big-business philanthropists, doing so much good, keeping their eye on things, not letting the money stray into the wrong hands."

"Well, you won't be in the their class."

He had a heartbreaking smile. It lit up his handsome dark face with its gilt-bronze tan. She wondered if he were a yachtsman. Most likely he was; that tan was from the sun, not any sunbed. "I don't want to be there when the will's read," she said with a faint shudder.

"I'll be there, too, Carol," he reassured her. "I expect I will have to go to the country house the day after tomorrow, maybe sooner. I'd like to take you with me. You should be there. The house is yours."

Her finely arched brows, so much darker than her hair, shot up. "You're serious?"

"Absolutely. Wills are serious matters."

"I know that." She coloured. "So I can tip them out— my uncle Maurice, Dallas and Troy, although he lives in the apartment at Point Piper. That belonged to Poppy." Her childhood name for her grandfather was flying out regardless.

"That remains with the family," he said. "Do you want to tip them out of Beaumont?"

She looked into his fathoms-deep dark eyes. "I have to think about that. I'm not finished my degree yet. I expect you've checked me out?" Of course he had. "I'm smart enough, apparently, but I'm not giving my studies my best shot."

"A fresh start next year," he suggested. "You'll feel more committed by then."

"Why were you so committed?" She really wanted to know. "We've all heard Professor Deakin sing your praises."

A faint grimace spread across his dynamic features. "I didn't have your advantages, Carol, but I've always wanted to be a lawyer. I was ambitious, an inherited trait. Then I, too, lost my dad, a geologist, when I was twelve."

So both of them had lost their fathers at an early age. He at twelve, she at age five. That made a bond.

"It was just my mother and me," he was saying. "I determined after that, it was my job to look after her, when she knew perfectly well how to look after both of us. She's a strong woman. She ran a very successful catering business until she sold out a year ago. These days she and her sister, my aunt Terri, travel the world."

"That's good. There would be so much to see." She hesitated for a moment before asking. "How did your father die? He wouldn't have been very old."

He told her, although he didn't talk much about the premature death of his father. "He died in a mine explosion in Chile where he had been sent by his company to explore copper deposits in the region. He was able to help get a lot of the men out. He wasn't so lucky. He was forty-one."

"Oh, Damon, I'm so sorry."

There was such a compassionate look on her face, he wanted to pull her to him.

Steady on!

Physical contact of the order he was thinking was out of the question. But even the thought gave him a strange pleasure that was very unsettling at the same time. He hadn't anticipated this feeling of urgency. Anyone would think he had been appointed her knight in shining armour.

"The long summer vacation is coming up," she said with a slight frown. "My Uncle Maurice made no attempt to see me in all these long years."

"No." She had been deprived of family.

"It's a heavy burden having a lot of money," she commented gravely.

"It is indeed. People don't always realize that. Money can't buy happiness. I've seen that time and time again. Too much money in a family can bring about a lot of internal conflict." A prominent family's feud was being publicly waged in the press at that point of time.

"Did my grandfather leave any instructions for me?" She hoped it was so.

"I'm glad you asked, Carol, because he did," he answered gently. "He wanted you to know how things were. He wanted you to know why certain decisions had to be made. I guess he wanted pardon."

"Then he's got it," she answered quietly. "I could never learn to hate my grandfather no matter what my mother tried to drum into me. I was a rebellious child, not easy to handle. Not cute at all. One thing in my favour—hate was left out of me, when sadly it defined my mother."

CHAPTER TWO

IN THE MORNING the news of Selwyn Chancellor's death broke on every TV channel and all over the internet. It didn't take long before the phones began to ring non-stop. Finally Carol let all the calls go to message. Even Tracey forgot her troubles, joining them for breakfast—possibly a mistake, because she had to endure exclamations of horror at the state of her face and neck from Amanda and Emma, as well as fierce comments on the low character of her ex-boyfriend, and the blood-curdling things they considered should be done to him. Finally Carol had to request them to stop.

"You got it, kiddo!" Amanda returned to lavishly buttering her toast, taking the spread meticulously to the edges. Satisfied, she spread it thickly with yeast extract. "My God, Caro, can you believe it?" She crunched a section in her mouth. "You're an heiress. If anyone deserves it, you do. But what are you going to do now? I mean, you won't be staying here. We won't be staying here, for that matter. Not without you. Can't afford it. What about Trace? She has to get out of her place. Her dumb-ass boyfriend might come back."

Carol shook her head. "Tracey will be taking out an apprehended-violence order on him within a day or two. None of you has to go anywhere. I'll be picking up the rent, although you can pay the phone and electricity. It will teach you how to mind your pennies." That was a shot at Amanda, who was always broke, always borrowing.

"That's a good one!" Amanda hooted with joy. "We have pennies. You'll have *millions!*"

"I know. The luck of the draw. But I'm going to do some good with it," Carol said with a zealot's fervour. "Are you availing yourself of my offer or not? I know quite a few who'd jump at the chance. Tracey can have my room. Does that suit, Trace?"

Tracey's expression was relieved beyond words. "Everyone needs a friend like you, Caro," she said with feeling. "Do you think Damon will remember about me?"

"Count on it." Carol placed a comforting hand on her shoulder. "He's a guy who makes time. He wouldn't miss a trick."

"And he's really your solicitor? I'm hugely envious."

"He is, for my sins."

Amanda gave a sly laugh, but Emma broke in naively. "Gosh, how thrilling! That guy has the wow factor!" She puckered her long nose. "You don't see guys who look like that every day. He's my idea of Mr Romance! I love those dark, brooding types. You should consider yourself a very lucky girl, Caro."

Carol did, but she wasn't about to admit to it. "Don't get excited over nothing, Em. I have no romantic notions about him. And I'm darn sure he doesn't have any about me."

"You'll have to do better than that, Caro." Amanda licked some spread off her fingers. "That guy would make even choosey little you jump for joy."

"I'll say!" Emma seconded with enthusiasm. "I'd kill for a guy like that. He could even make me his love slave."

Amanda nearly choked. "All those romances you devour by the basketload have got to you, Em. They're just fairytales. They should come with a warning: *this isn't for real.*"

"Is, too!" said Emma doggedly. "Our Mary got the Crown Prince of Denmark."

"By virtue of the fact she looks more royal than the royals," Amanda chortled.

No one was going to argue with that.

By the time they finished breakfast, all was settled. Amanda was given the job of roping in a couple of fellow students to help Tracey move out of her flat, while Carol wrote a cheque to cover two weeks of Tracey's rent in advance.

Tracey burst into tears.

Carol didn't spend long on the phone talking to her mother. She had found out the hard way she couldn't trust her.

"Why didn't you tell me Poppy wanted custody of me?" she asked with a feeling of great sadness.

"Stop using that ridiculous name," Roxanne fired back. She'd been wondering for years when the truth would out. "He wanted no such thing. He was just as mean as ever a man could be."

"You're lying, Roxanne." Her mother had insisted on being called by her first name for years now. *"Mum"* was considered indecently ageing.

"Think what you like." Roxanne made a rude yawning sound. "You're not going to his funeral, are you? It's a mystery to me why anyone would turn up."

"It's a private funeral at Beaumont," Carol was glad to point out. "I'm going with my solicitor. It appears Poppy has included me in his will."

A moment of silence, then Roxanne let out a screech that would have done justice to a cockatoo in the wild. *"He what?"*

"Ah, you're shocked." Carol felt pleased. "It appears he thought of me at the end. At the beginning, too, as I've recently found out. I bet he paid for my uni tuition and my car?" she hazarded, intuiting it could be true. It was her mother who was mean. "You're not invited, Mother. Neither is Jeff. A decision I'm entirely in agreement with. I've always known you tried to poison my mind against my grandfather."

Roxanne's laugh was low and derisive. "Just because he's remembered you doesn't mean you're going to get much. Your grandfather was quite eccentric. Maurice, pathetic failure that he is, and that moon-faced wife of his—she's totally descended into a frump—will get the bulk of it. Troy will get the rest after all the tax breaks—the charities—get their share. If you're lucky, he might leave you some of those God-awful Chinese pots." She laughed again, as though enjoying a huge joke. "I never told you I deliberately broke one before I left. I had an overwhelming urge to destroy something as I walked out of the entrance hall. You were already in the car. It was very valuable, I believe."

"Not the blue-and-white *meiping* vase?" Carol gasped. It had stood in the hallway on a tall rosewood stand.

"What the hell? Your grandfather neglected to take me on as a pupil, so I wouldn't know, except I couldn't help noticing his face went white as the vase hit the marble tiles. The man was really obsessed. He had far too many vases and pots as it was. Who the hell did he think he was, Ali Baba? When is the funeral?" she asked. "When are you leaving?"

"Is it vital to know?"

"Don't get smart with me," Roxanne warned.

"It's what I always am, remember? But, to answer your question, I'm waiting on a phone call."

"Do you feel sad?" Roxanne gave a heartless coo.

"I do, actually. It must be strange being you—completely indifferent to anyone else's pain but hyper-sensitive about yourself."

"I don't know what you're talking about." Roxanne reacted angrily to criticism. "I do know all you ever did even as a child was try to wind me up. Do give my love to dearest Maurice. Never had the guts to get rid of Dallas," she added quite bitterly.

That was news indeed to Carol. "Did he want to get rid of her?" she asked, astonished.

"You bet he did!" was Roxanne's startling reply.

"Well, well…" Carol was having a job absorbing this further piece of news. "My solicitor isn't Marcus Bradfield, by the way. It's another member of the firm, Damon Hunter."

Roxanne gave a follow-up shriek. "You're having me on. Damon Hunter?"

"You know him?" It was very possible. Her mother and Jeff attended just about everything.

"I know *of* him." Roxanne shifted into honeyed tones. "We haven't as yet met but I've seen him at various functions. Hard to miss, really. He's going with Amber Coleman at the moment. The betting is she'll get him to the altar. Gorgeous-looking man. Very sleek. Reminds me of a glossy black panther. Don't imagine for a minute he'd be interested in you, my dear. Amber is *magnificent,* a real love goddess."

"Who flunked university."

Roxanne laughed. "Dumb of you to think a beautiful woman needs a university education."

"Easy for an airhead to catch a man—miracle for her to hold on to him," Carol returned. "Bye now, Mother."

"You let me know what happens." Roxanne returned to her hectoring tones.

"I'll call the minute I know."

Roxanne registered the sarcasm. "Don't you forget, young lady, how good I was to you. You had the best of everything—your precious education, your car."

"I won't say thanks, because I now suspect that was Poppy."

"Go to hell!" said Roxanne.

* * *

Carol was doing her best to control her emotions. But, now that they were well into their journey, she could feel the panic coming. The family once the will was read would hate her all the more. Not that they had ever loved her.

Her father had loved her. She realised now her mother had always been jealous of her in a way. When she'd been a child her father had doted on her—possibly to the exclusion of his wife? Roxanne was one of those women who demanded all attention be focused on her. She wasn't sure her parents had been happy. She remembered the arguments even from when she'd been a little girl. Her mother was a very volatile person. Her memory told her it was her mother who had initiated the shouting matches. Nothing had ever suited her mother, even when she was living in such affluence. In retrospect Carol considered it a miracle the marriage had lasted as long as it did. Her parents appeared to have been hopelessly *mismatched*. She thought it was a word she had overheard her grandfather once use.

They had been driving for around forty minutes, so they weren't that far off the estate. It was situated in the Southern Highlands of the state, some three-thousand feet above sea level; an area of spectacular beauty, with a cool temperate climate, less than seventy kilometres south-west of Sydney. The region was known not only for its breathtaking scenery but its beautiful parks and gardens and the many stately mansions built in much earlier times as summer retreats for the wealthy. The National Park, with its waterfalls and limestone caves, offered great walking tracks, look-outs and picnic facilities.

Probably the most attractive town in the area was the garden town of Bowral, not far from the estate. The town was also home to the Bradman Museum with a bronze statue of Sir Donald Bradman right outside. Her father had once taken a photo of her sitting on the plinth at Sir Donald's feet. He told her Sir Donald had been the greatest batsman of all time. She remembered Tulip Time, too. It was a town festival that lasted for a couple of weeks when thousands upon thousands of tulips came into exquisite bloom. She always bought tulips in season to this day.

"You're very quiet," Damon commented after a while.

She turned her head to look at him. He had a very striking profile; finely chiselled straight nose, the firm, clean-cut jaw and above all the mouth. She imagined what it would be like to be kissed by that mouth. She had to turn away. Physical attraction, she was forced to consider, was a very real thing. She wondered if he might be attracted to her. She expected he would consider her far too young for his tastes. It was in those dark eyes when they fell on her: *just a baby.*

She looked down at her hands in her lap. "Memories. I find myself getting caught up in them. I have to admit to a sinking feeling in the pit of my stomach. I know the family is going to bitterly resent me. Amanda's parting advice, was *'watch your back.'* It's still ringing in my ears."

"Carol, the will is airtight. They can resent all they like. Your grandfather left the bulk of his personal fortune to you. I should point out your uncle and your cousin, Troy, have been very handsomely provided for. Your grandfather was, after all, a very rich man."

"What about Dallas?" Carol remembered her uncle's wife as a good-looking, dark-haired woman, but not kind, at least to her. Dallas's one soft spot was for her son, Troy, older than Carol by six years.

"Dallas doesn't get a mention," Damon told her. "Which suggests the marriage won't break down. Your aunt by marriage has always been extremely well looked-after."

"So who's going to run everything now that my grandfather is gone? Who is fit to step into his shoes? *I* can't, for heaven's sake."

"No one is expecting you to," he said gently. "But at some point you will want a seat on the board. Lew Hoffman, your grandfather's right-hand man, will step into the role. He's a very capable man, very highly regarded. The board will eventually vote on chairman and CEO. I would expect Hoffman will remain in place, at least for the foreseeable future."

"And how will Uncle Maurice feel about that?"

"Relieved, I would think." His tone was dry. Everyone in the city knew Maurice Chancellor didn't have a head for business.

A sharp bend, then a tree-lined road straight ahead: it led directly to Beaumont, the Chancellor country estate.

"The estate wasn't always in the family," Carol said. "My great-grandfather bought it some time in the late 1940s."

"I knew that."

"Did you? Silly of me—you would have done your homework. He saved the once-splendid Victorian residence from the wreckers' ball. The original family had lost sons to two world wars, after which the estate went into a serious decline."

"As did the fortunes and the lifestyle of the Wickhams," Damon supplied.

"How sad." Carol felt echoes of their pain. "At least my great-grandfather saved the estate."

"Legend has it he paid the Wickhams beyond the asking price."

"That's good to hear. How did you find out?"

He shot her an amused glance. "Fairly common knowledge, Carol, at least in the legal world." God, how she delighted his eye! No getting away from it. If she were a few years older, and not Selwyn Chancellor's granddaughter and his client, he would make it his business to get to know her *much* better.

She was wearing a very pretty dress, very feminine—an upmarket sundress, wide straps over her shoulders, tiny bodice, full skirt, with white sandals on her feet. *I didn't want to wear anything black.* In her pink flower-sprigged white dress she was springtime. Her whole aura reflected the flower world. She had pulled her glowing mane back into a Grecian knot showing off her delicately carved features and the length of her slender neck. He hadn't forgotten what she had told him about her cousin, Troy. He could well imagine Troy Chancellor lusting after her, cousin or not.

"Well, I didn't know," she was saying. "But then there's lots I don't know. My great-grandfather hired the finest architect of the day to restore the house. He made extensive additions in the form of the two wings to either side."

He nodded. "It gave the original house rather regal dimensions."

"I knew my way around it," she said proudly, remembering the little girl she'd been. She was finding it so easy to talk to him, when she rarely if ever confided family matters to others. "It was supposed to be a happy house in my great-grandfather's day, a happy house in the early years of my grandfather's tenure. Then happiness seemed to have fallen away. Even as a child I was aware my gentle grandmother, Elaine, had issues. I was never able to plumb the depth of them, but as an adult I've interpreted some of those issues as extreme shyness. She could even have been mildly autistic. There's an avenue I will have to look into as a charity, now that I'm in a position to do so."

He knew she meant it and found it admirable. "Not the most helpful characteristics for the wife of a highly successful man destined to go higher," he observed gently.

Carol gave a sigh. "My grandmother always lived at Beaumont. She shunned the city except on those special occasions when Poppy talked her into it. The coup de grâce, the final blow, came with the death of my father. My grandmother retreated from life. She retreated from everyone including me. Finally she chose to end it. Maybe my family is cursed." She turned her head so she could register his response.

"Not many families escape tragedy, Carol," he said, looking straight ahead at the sun-dappled road. "You're not cursed. You have a very bright future. You're going to study hard in your final year. You'll gain a first-class degree. I have it on good authority you will, if you work. You're going to need a legal background in the years ahead. Increasingly you'll be in a position of power."

"You already are," she pointed out rather dryly. "You have power over *me*."

Massive black wrought-iron gates soared to some ten feet. They were closed. She gave a wry laugh. "Looks like they don't want us to come in. Never mind—I'll open the gates." She had one hand on the door of the car.

"Carol, no need." He stopped her. "I'll call through to the house."

"Hey, that's new," she said, sighting for the first time the impressive-looking button-entry intercom panel. It was set into a stone pillar, with a stone pineapple on top.

Damon lowered his window and punched in a five-digit code. Afterwards he told Carol the code.

"I got it the first time," she said. She was very good with numbers.

"You're sharp."

"Indeed I am, Damon Hunter, so remember." Her glance was blue flame.

"There should be a lot more security on the house," he said seriously. "There are places anyone could—"

He broke off as a woman's flatish voice came through the speaker. "Who is this, please?"

"Identify yourself, Damon," Carol joked sternly.

He threw her a half smile. It made really sexy little brackets to frame his mouth. "Damon Hunter with my client, Carol Emmett. I rang ahead."

There was no reply, but the huge gates started to open inwards.

"Good to know we're welcome," Carol spoke dryly. "It's a big comfort to have your support, Damon." He had such a strong presence. "That wasn't the lady of the house."

"No, it's the housekeeper, Amy Hoskins. She's not Mrs Danvers, but she's definitely channelling her."

Carol recognised the name as that of the daunting housekeeper in Daphne Du Maurier's famous novel *Rebecca*. "I guess I could fire her, come to that. I've read *Rebecca* twice. Never could find a copy of the movie. Mrs Hoskins sounds like she's taken a set against me already." She spoke lightly, when her stomach was knotted with nerves.

"Then, as you say, she can go. You own this house, Carol, the entire estate. You own the house at Point Piper. Your uncle retains the Point Piper apartment where your cousin lives at the present time."

"The house at Point Piper?" Carol gasped in dismay. "Whatever would I do with that? I don't want all this money. All these possessions. The Point Piper house is a city icon. It must be worth…" She couldn't begin to guess.

"Around fifty million dollars even in these depressed times."

She drew in her breath. "That kind of money is obscene. How can any house outside a palace or one of the great stately homes of England and Europe be worth that kind of money?"

"Well, it does have a magnificent view of Sydney Harbour," he said dryly. "Which means arguably the finest view in the world. I happen to know your grandfather was approached last year by a Chinese businessman based in Hong Kong. I believe he has a comparable house on Victoria Peak. Of course, it doesn't have a bad view, either."

Like *Rebecca*'s nameless heroine, she couldn't believe she was back. She couldn't believe all this was hers. It would take ages and ages for it to sink in. The extensive parklike grounds, and beyond them the woodlands, were filled with large numbers of exotic trees and indigenous gums. She caught a glimpse of the man-made lake through the clearings. Anyone coming onto the property would have thought it a natural lagoon, only natural lagoons didn't occur in the area. She remembered the wonderful tree ferns that grew around the verge, the great clumps of white arum lilies and Japanese iris.

She had been an observant little girl, with a great love of nature, both her father and her grandfather had fostered. Her grandmother, too, on her good days. Carol wasn't a bad artist, either. She had painted the abstract in the flat in a single Saturday afternoon. Even she thought it looked good—which wasn't to say she was a real painter, but she did have talent. Her art teacher at her very good girls' school—Guy Morris, a recognised artist himself—had tried hard to encourage her but she couldn't seem to concentrate on any one thing in those days.

The house lay ahead. Even after her long years of absence it looked just the same; time might have stopped. The gravelled driveway encircled a focal point, the big beautiful Victorian fountain with its pond raised high above ground, the three-tiered fountain higher. The fountain in turn was surrounded by a gravelled walk. Around the walk, borders of lush green lawn some two feet wide made a striking foil for the prolifically flowering rose gardens. In this area of the gardens, fronting the house, the beds hosted only the colour pink, from the blush pinks through the salmon pinks to the deepest rose pink. It suited the rose-coloured bricks used in the house's construction and the deep-blue shutters. That had been her grandmother Elaine's idea. She clearly remembered one late afternoon when all had been quiet, her grandmother taking her by the hand for a stroll around the playing fountain that set sparkling jets of water cascading down into the pool.

Her grandmother had not thrived like her roses.

"Too much to expect the welcome mat. What now?" They stood out on the gravelled drive, looking up at the house. The high and wide front door, framed by very elegant acid etched side and fan lights, was shut.

"We proceed." He took her arm, tall and commanding, with born authority. It was a huge asset, Carol thought. Damon was in control.

As they moved up the short flight of stone steps, the panelled front door opened to admit them.

"Maybe she thought we were going to storm in?" Carol whispered, seeing some humour in the situation.

A tall broad-hipped woman in a slate-blue outfit with a white collar—clearly a uniform—stood there. Not to greet them, precisely; there was no welcoming smile on her face, not even a civil spread of the lips. It was a bit too early for smiles, perhaps.

"Good afternoon, Mrs Hoskins." Damon took charge.

"Good afternoon, Mr Hunter. Ms Emmett," the housekeeper responded, her glance whipping over Carol from head to foot, fixing onto the ruby-red hair as though the colour was not to her taste.

"I take it the family are already assembled?" Damon asked.

The woman suddenly looked flustered, her cheeks turning

red. "Mr Maurice is in the library. Mr Troy hasn't as yet arrived from the city. Mrs Chancellor will be down presently."

"Then perhaps you can show us into the library," Damon
suggested. "I don't have a great deal of time."

"Certainly, Mr Hunter." She straightened her shoulders.
"Would you care for tea or coffee?"

"Carol?" Damon turned to her. She looked porcelain-pale,
otherwise composed. This would be a traumatic time for her.

"Coffee would be nice. Thank you, Mrs Hoskins." Carol's answer was brisk, not impolite, but rather like someone
who had grown up with lots of people to look after her. *To
the manor born,* Damon thought wryly, to put a pun on the
original *'manner.'* But then, she had been manor born and
her mother and stepfather lived in considerable style. "I know
my way to the library. We'll go through."

The housekeeper's head came up, as if affronted by this
red-headed youngster taking charge. "I should announce
you."

"We'll announce ourselves." Carol's reply was very direct.
Damon didn't have to utter a word.

The housekeeper put a hand to her forehead, then for a
well-built woman made a mouselike scurry away.

"I take it you've started out as you mean to go on?" Damon
asked with amusement.

Her gaze flashed to his. "Don't have much alternative, do
I? If they think they're going to intimidate me, they've got
another think coming."

"Slowly, slowly, catchee monkey," he cautioned.

She knew he was trying to calm her. "I thought it was
'softly, softly, catchee monkey'? Where did the expression
come from anyway?" she asked, her eyes ranging over the
familiar furnishings of the imposing entrance hall. The rosewood stand that had once held the *meiping* vase her mother
had smashed now held a lesser Chinese porcelain vase. "Ob-

viously somewhere people wanted to catch monkeys. India, Asia?"

"It would have to refer to British colonial rule," Damon said. "I've read some say the founder of the Boy Scouts, Lord Robert Baden-Powell when he was stationed in Ghana. Others say soldiers posted to the Far East often wanted to catch monkeys as pets. Snaring them must have taken a lot of patience. Either way, I think we can adopt it as a guiding principle, Carol."

"Especially when one comes into some serious money."

He quietly laughed.

They found Maurice Chancellor in the library, the core of the house. He was seated in a magnificent Russian Empire armchair that had carved and gilded front legs in the form of a lion's head and paws. Carol remembered how her grandfather had told her the gilded lion symbolised power. So her uncle was making a statement. The library was a very large, handsome room in which a series of tall mahogany bookcases were set into niches. A pair of large early nineteenth-century terrestrial and celestial globes on stands stood to either side of the near doorway. A magnificent room-sized Indian Agra rug with an all-over floral design covered the floor, the field dark ruby-red, the border green. A George IV rosewood library table with an inset green leather writing surface stood beneath a splendid bronze and Baccarat crystal chandelier with a seven-foot drop.

The moment they entered the room, Maurice Chancellor stood up.

Her uncle. Her father's younger brother.

She would have recognised him anywhere. He was very like her father, tall and handsome with a full head of hair, once a dark red but faded to tawny, with the contrasting dark brows Carol herself possessed. Of course he was much older now. His blue eyes were hooded and he had put on weight, but he was still a strikingly handsome man. He came towards them, a welcoming figure, a smile on a generous mouth, perhaps a shade slack.

It was a well-calculated act, Damon thought, well used to people who thought they had power. Power tended to lend a lot of arrogance and snobbery. He was instantly on the alert, instantly protective.

"My dear girl, welcome home!" Maurice Chancellor's voice was a deep, dark cultured purr. "Hunter." He transferred his gaze momentarily to acknowledge Damon.

He was all *bon homie.*

It should have been reassuring, only for a paralysing moment Carol was overcome by panic. Panic didn't even cover the way she felt. Her uncle was smiling at her, yet she felt terror. The terror of a child. Like a curtain in a theatre, the curtain in her mind was trying to go up, only to drop back heavily. Memories; memories were inevitably overlain by what happened afterwards in life.

Acutely attuned to her reactions, Damon moved to stand at her shoulder. He was so close to her he was able to record the nervous tremors in her body. He thought her reaction strange. It was as though she was frozen on the spot. Perhaps it was understandable, but most unexpected. She was such a spirited young woman. Hadn't he been witness to her mettle when she'd been fronting a dangerous thug?

Just as he started to get concerned, she shrugged the moment off. *Gone.* She looked up at him for a moment as if to say *I'm okay,* then she moved forward with balletic grace to meet her uncle.

"Uncle Maurice." Her clear voice was full of a sardonic self-assurance. "Such a very long time since I've seen you— what, fifteen years? It's taken Grandfather's passing to redress that. Please accept my sincere sympathy."

Maurice Chancellor looked momentarily taken aback. As

well he might be. He fancied he saw a lot of both his father and his brother in his niece. "Sad times," he acknowledged, producing a suitably sombre tone. "Sad times."

"All I can think of is how much I missed out on seeing my grandfather," Carol replied, knowing now she had her own mother to thank for that.

"Terrible way to treat you," Maurice Chancellor said with more than a smidgeon of shame.

As Carol somehow dreaded he might, he took her by the shoulders, bending to kiss her on both cheeks. He smelled of cigars, the most expensive kind, and a faintly cloying cologne. "Come, sit down," he bid them, the suave host, turning to include Damon. "A good trip?" he asked.

"No problems," Damon responded, trying to decode what was going on. Maurice Chancellor was play-acting; he was certain of that. Damon was proud of Carol. He was strongly on side, as he had been from the beginning. Given a little time, he thought she would develop into a remarkable young woman. She *had* to. She would have huge responsibilities.

"I'll have Mrs Hoskins bring—what?—tea or coffee? Both?" Maurice Chancellor looked from one to the other, waving them into a couple of very grand chairs.

"I've already told Mrs Hoskins we'd like coffee, Uncle Maurice," Carol said. "How long do you think we'll have to wait for Dallas and Troy? We have to return to Sydney after the will is read. Mr Hunter has numerous commitments, as you can imagine." There was a further barely detectable sting in the tail.

"Of course, of course." The indulgent smile slipped a little. In the world Maurice Chancellor frequented, no one talked down to him or even treated him like an equal. His niece was doing that now, albeit in a polished way. It didn't fool him at all. It came to him that she had been an exceptional little girl, much smarter than his son. The stand-out grandchild, just as her father, Adam, had been the stand-out son. What a hell of a role he'd had to play in life, always second best.

He turned to Damon Hunter who was fast gaining an impressive reputation in the city. He had come with Marcus Bradfield's full recommendation, though he wasn't as yet a partner. He was young yet, but it was just a matter of time. Hunter was the embodiment of all the things his son, Troy, was not. Hunter was waiting courteously until Carol was seated in a mahogany leather-buttoned armchair that swallowed her up before he took a wing chair near her. "Why did my father never tell me he had *you* handle his last will and testament, instead of Marcus Bradfield?" Maurice asked, beetling his dark brows.

"I expect he settled on me after I proved helpful in other areas," Damon offered by way of explanation.

"He always did the unexpected, my father." There was a faint note of unease in Maurice's tone. "Ah, here's Dallas!" He broke off as a woman in late middle age entered the room. Both Carol and Damon stood up respectfully.

Neither the open door nor the warm welcome. With a spasm of regret, Carol registered how her aunt by marriage had physically gone downhill. Dallas couldn't hold a candle to her mother—never could have—but she had been an attractive woman. Sadly, she hadn't been looking after herself.

Dallas Chancellor flashed them both a steely glance and a curt nod. She stood well back. "Good afternoon," she said as though determined not to say another word.

Now, here's the interesting bit, Carol thought. *At least I know where I am with Dallas.* Dallas wasn't going to make a grand show of fussing. There would be no happy huggermugger encounter, she thought in relief. Her mother had passed the remark that Dallas had turned into *'a frump.'* Dallas unfortunately had. She had grown surprisingly chunky, when Carol remembered her as having been slim. But she was still expensively dressed, not a hair on her head out of place. These days her hair was an indescribable colour—maybe beige. Two things stood out: husband and wife weren't in perfect accord. And Dallas wasn't going to play her husband's game.

Carol and Damon responded with a good afternoon. They threw themselves into their allotted roles.

"Troy not here yet?" Dallas addressed her husband as though she suspected he had locked their son in a cupboard.

"My dear, have you ever known Troy to be on time for anything?" Maurice Chancellor replied with gentle mockery, but surely it was hostility that leaked from his eyes?

Just as Dallas was about to reply, the housekeeper came to the door, pushing a laden trolley on rubber wheels. Dallas, who had taken a seat at the library table, signalled her in as if to say 'let's get this over.' As she did so, she sent one of the leather-bound books on the rosewood table flying.

Damon bent to retrieve it, noticing a photograph that had been lying between the pages fly out then glide under the table. He decided he'd rescue it later. He'd seen only a flash, but he'd registered the photograph was of a very pretty girl, perhaps sixteen, wearing the uniform of a prestige girls' school. Who had taken the photograph then placed it inside a book? He thought Carol might like to know.

Carol had noticed the flight of the photograph but had only seen the back. She gave him a quick look. He answered with the slightest movement of his dark head.

Over coffee and delicious little cupcakes Dallas Chancellor managed a passing semblance to a hostess, if not a close relative. "You haven't grown tall, Carol," she said in a fit of bitchiness. She stared at her husband's niece as if it would take Carol a lifetime to attain a reasonable height.

Not a promising start, but Carol was undismayed. She

could have made the comment that Dallas had piled on the kilos but she kept that to herself. She considered herself too well-bred, though most of what she had learned of etiquette was out of books. Roxanne had been anything but a hands-on mother.

Maurice Chancellor, however, showed dismay. He threw up his beautifully manicured hands—obviously no hard physical labour there, beyond opening out the ironed newspaper. "My dear, Carol looks absolutely beautiful. She's petite, like my mother."

"Let's hope she doesn't take after her," Dallas sniffed. Dallas had made a point of getting in the last word for many years now.

The housekeeper had returned to collect cups, saucers and plates and was wheeling the trolley away just as Troy turned up. There were no apologies for being late, rather a sneering laugh. "Home is where the family gathers," he announced, making a beeline for Carol. He was wearing a very expensive business suit, a blinding white shirt with a natty stripped tie. He wasn't as tall as his father, nor as handsome. His eyes had the granite-grey sheen of his mother's. He leaned over Carol, virtually trapping her, bending his smooth brown head to kiss her on the cheek.

"*You're* here, Caro, that's all I care about. You look ravishing, as usual. Hi there, Damon." He threw a challenging glance at Damon, as though they were both contenders for Carol's hand. "I see a huge career boost happening for you."

"It's long since underway." Damon hadn't liked that kiss. He felt so strongly about it, his response were something of a shock. It definitely wasn't a familial kiss. "Now we're all here, I'd like to start reading the will," he said, knowing the contents would cause a sensation. He thought if it was up to her closest relatives Carol might have a very short life span.

That cried out for protection. He was in place, if not her knight in shining armour, her guardian angel in his own way.

"We're certainly not stopping you." Troy spoke facetiously, looking mightily pleased with himself. He had taken a chair to the other side of Carol, slinging a hand over its arm. Again, not a cousinly gesture. What was he thinking? They were first cousins; their fathers were brothers. Or did he think the rules had changed entirely? He could have been a young man making marriage plans.

"So the old guy finally thought of you," Troy murmured to Carol, leaning in very close.

"Why don't you shut up, Troy?" she responded.

Not the most affectionate of answers, Damon thought, well pleased. He moved into lawyer mode, allowing gravitas to enter his voice. "I would ask you all to remain quiet so you can pay attention. When you're ready, I'll proceed."

"Let's reap the whirlwind!" Troy cried. "There's a lot at stake. Oh, yeah!" he exclaimed flippantly, giving a long, relaxed yawn. His mother and father, however, were looking extremely tense. His mother was thinking long and hard about whether she'd be in a good position to leave his father, no doubt, Troy thought. Theirs was not a marriage made in heaven. Come to think of it, how many were? Troy couldn't wait to get the hell out of there. His dad would get the lion's share; that didn't bother him. He would get enough for the time being. It would *all* come to him in the end. He had no special problem with Carol getting a share. She was a gorgeous little thing and as sexy as hell! As far as he knew, it was perfectly legal to get hitched to one's first cousin, especially with different mothers.

What followed was either farce or high tragedy. Carol, the one the family had turned their back on, the principal beneficiary? My God, what a turn up!

"You've got the whole damned kit and caboodle." Troy, like his mother and father, showed his stupefaction.

"This is horrible, *horrible!*" Dallas jumped to her feet, looking like a minor volcano about to erupt. "I'm dreaming, aren't I? Selwyn left the bulk of his personal fortune to Carol? Why, she knows nothing of the world. Nothing!" She struck the library table with her clenched fist. "Don't sit there like a trout with your mouth open, Maurice. Say something. We have to fight this. Selwyn clearly wasn't of sound mind."

"My father was of sound mind from start to finish," Maurice said with some bitterness. He was making a real effort to bite down on his shock. He'd had a lifetime of being bypassed. He had never received his due. At least the old man had left him with a sizeable fortune. It was no surprise Dallas wasn't on the list. He'd knock her off *his* list if only he could. But she knew where the bodies were buried. He and his brother, Adam, had had poor judgement when it came to women. His son, Troy, who gave himself such airs and graces, thoroughly deserved a good set-down. Not that Troy was going short, either.

Troy didn't agree. "This is outrageous, a bloody knock-out blow." For once Troy sided with his mother. "Carol not only takes precedence over you, Dad, she takes precedence over me." Obviously the more serious blow. "He always was a ruthless old bastard. You know what this is all about? It's *spite.* He let us all believe we would inherit in the usual way. I *am* your heir, Dad. He never did like Mother dear. Don't you remember he never would drink any of your herbal concoctions, Mother? Wasn't *My Cousin Rachel* one of your favourite books? No, the old man didn't trust Mother any more than he trusted that psycho bitch, Roxanne."

Carol, who had been sitting stunned by the magnitude of her inheritance and the attendant responsibilities, spoke up.

"I'd appreciate it if you didn't target my mother, Troy," she said sharply.

"Do you want to know the truth?" Troy all but yelled.

"Perhaps you could sit down, Troy. You, too, Mrs Chancellor," Damon intervened in the sort of voice one obeyed. "Over these last years Selwyn Chancellor became more and more concerned about how his granddaughter had been treated. We don't have to touch on the furore after Carol's father's tragic death. Mr Chancellor had wanted custody of Carol, but our best advice was the court wouldn't take her from her mother."

"News to me!" Maurice Chancellor pronounced. "We all know what part my sister-in-law played in my brother's death."

Damon saw Carol flinch. "I would remind you, Mr Chancellor, the coroner brought in a verdict of accidental drowning."

"You mean she was never found out!" Dallas cried, pathologically jealous of her former sister-in-law.

"There are laws against slander," Damon reminded them quietly. "Roxanne Chancellor's story was accepted. There are always accidents on boats."

There was a chilling malice from Dallas. "My husband is right. Roxanne was never to be trusted." Bucket loads of aggression were in her tone.

Troy flopped down in his chair, looking poleaxed. It wasn't as though he would have to cut back on his living expenses; it was the sheer unfairness of it all. The loss of face. He suspected his father would adapt to his new situation given time. All his father could aspire to was writing a book. He had wanted to for years—a work of fiction, a potential blockbuster, no less. A bit late in the day! The only catch was his father loved Beaumont with a passion. He would bitterly resent being thrown out of the family home, a home he had confidently expected to be his. Carol's position could be seen as hazardous.

All Selwyn Chancellor's pet charities got a huge slice, as expected, so too medical research, the arts, the State Art Gallery, the museum, endowments to the state university, legacies to this one and that one, loyal henchmen. The old devil had even left a hefty sum to the Dairy Farmers' Association, for God's sake.

"Save the cows!" Troy cried. "I bet they'll be delighted."

"When are we expected to move out?" Dallas asked with barely banked molten rage. When his mother made a point, she wanted people really to feel it. It was a mystery to Troy his parents hadn't split up. His father was still a very handsome man, whereas his mother had taken some kind of savage pleasure in letting herself go.

Carol took a moment to answer. "There's absolutely no hurry. I intend to keep a low profile, or as low as I can get. I intend to complete my law degree, which will be at the end of next year. The house is big enough for all of us, should I decide to spend time here—which, I must tell you, I will—long weekends, vacations, that sort of thing. And, before you ask, you have the use of the Point Piper house until I sell it."

Dallas reared back as though she'd been walloped. *"Sell?"* The sheer audacity of the girl! Had she no respect? Her solid body shook as if hit by successive earthquake tremors.

Troy in his turn muttered a violent oath.

"That's the idea," Carol continued calmly. "It will take time for me, with the help of Mr Hunter and others, to study my grandfather's wishes. As we saw from his will, my grandfather remained a great philanthropist to the end."

"Ah, yes, the great man in public. Something very different in private," Maurice Chancellor lamented.

"I saw far too little of him to judge," Carol replied. "I consider I have a responsibility passed on to me, public or otherwise, to do good in this world."

"Good?" Troy had become as pugnacious as his mother. "Why don't you open the house to the starving homeless?" he suggested wildly. "Or turn it into a holy place and give it to the Church. What about a holiday home for the Dalai Lama? What the hell are you on about, Carol? Do you have the faintest idea what that modest little pile is worth?"

"It so happens she does, Troy," Damon broke in, in a voice that halted any further inquiry. "Carol is not here to answer questions."

Troy backed off, still glaring his defiance.

"This is a nightmare!" Dallas exclaimed, desperately wishing for Carol to disappear to parts unknown. "What on earth am I going to tell my friends?"

"What friends, Mother?" Troy asked quite viciously.

"Blessings on you, too, dear." Dallas shot him a fierce broadside.

"Mind how you speak to your mother, Troy," Maurice Chancellor intervened half-heartedly. He was sick to death of the two of them, wife and son. They gave him no respect, no affection.

Damon began to push Selwyn Chancellor's last will and testament with its copy into his briefcase, allowing a couple of loose sheets of paper to fall onto the magnificent carpet. "Litigation is out of the question," he said quietly as he bent to retrieve them. "My client is Selwyn Chancellor's daughter by his elder son, his heir. It's fitting, given the past, that reparation be made."

"And what circumstances would that be?" Dallas demanded, howling her shock and rage, as good as any theatrical performance.

Damon fixed his brilliant dark eyes on her. "I would think you would know, Mrs Chancellor. As a family, you did not support her. It will take time for Carol to see her way clearly. She will get every support from me and others appointed by her grandfather. My client has told me in advance she is prepared to be reasonable in all matters. I would suggest the family present a united front to avoid a media circus. We all know there will be a blaze of publicity when it's known Carol is her grandfather's principal beneficiary."

Damon moved. With his height, he was towering over Dallas who stood looking up at him, her cheeks jiggling with wrath. "We don't need any lectures from you, young man."

"Correction—Ms Chancellor's solicitor and financial adviser," he said blandly. "Bradfield Douglass will want to keep the family's business. The fortune remains in the family, only there has been a redistribution."

"Revenge!" Dallas shook a raised fist. She was in a highly emotional state. "That's what it's all about." She let her long-suffering resentment rip. "There's still a possibility we can fight this…this…*warped* will."

"Frankly, Mrs Chancellor," Damon said, "You don't stand a chance. Many thanks for afternoon tea. Time for us to be getting back to town. If you have any further questions in the days ahead, I'll be happy to answer them. Interment is on Friday afternoon at 2:00 p.m. A few close friends and colleagues of Mr Chancellor will attend. They've been advised—all are coming. A memorial service will be held in St Mary's Cathedral in Sydney Wednesday of next week, as you know. A caterer has been appointed to take charge of the small reception after the interment. They'll arrive before midday from Sydney. At this sad time, my client wanted to take that small burden off the family."

Dallas's steely eyes flashed. "Don't you just love her? She's all *heart*." Her voice was so harsh she might have had a scouring pad stuck in her throat.

"You would be wise to be grateful, Mrs Chancellor," Damon said in clipped professional tones.

"I'll see you out," Maurice Chancellor announced, waving an arm in the general direction of the front door. Obviously he intended continuing on in the role of legitimate master of Beaumont.

"Thank you, Uncle Maurice," Carol said.

CHAPTER THREE

THE INTERMENT WAS a harrowing experience. Everyone was glad when it was over, but mercifully a brilliant sun shone down on them. There was a point when Carol thought she just might cave in on herself. Scenes from the past began to invade her mind: the happy times with her grandfather; picking him flowers before he left for the city; the occasional but delightful walks she had enjoyed with her gentle little grandmother who had not been cut out for the life she had married into.

Damon had given her a photograph of herself as a schoolgirl. It had been taken outside the front gates of her school. Who else but her grandfather would have taken it, or caused it to be taken? It was the photograph Damon had retrieved after it had fallen out of a book that first day at Beaumont. He had guessed correctly she would want to have it. Perhaps there were lots of other photographs. She knew she would go in search of them; such mementoes were very important to her now.

Know that I loved you, Poppy. Know that I loved you, Nona. Know that I love you, Daddy.

The memories were tumbling freely. She felt a tremendous weight of regret. But she was in a different time now, a different space. There was only today.

Her grandfather had been much taken by the fact Franklin

Delano Roosevelt, the great American President, had been buried in his mother's rose garden at Springwood, the Roosevelt family estate. That set a precedent for Selwyn. He and his Elaine lay side by side, finding a closeness that had eluded them in life. Her mother, who had a hide any rhinoceros might covet, actually turned up with her husband, Jeff, who did the driving. Roxanne delighted in throwing the cat among the pigeons.

Jeff looking very sleek and prosperous gave Carol a wry smile and a too-intimate hug, near crushing her body to him. One had to wonder what secret feelings were lurking beneath Jeff's affable exterior.

"Let go, Jeff," she said briefly, wanting to kick him.

"Sweetheart, I'm just so pleased to see you. You never call. You never ring."

"Gosh, I wonder why?"

Her mother spoke like a woman forever doomed to be misunderstood. "Your father was my *husband,* Carol." A perfectly good reason for her presence, apparently. Roxanne was looking marvellous, but wearing a sweet, spicy perfume that was making Carol feel a bit sick.

"Husband number one," Carol said.

Roxanne countered. "How long do I have to suffer your flip remarks? I have a right to be here, Carol. I'm your mother."

Her tone riled, but Carol kept control. Too many people were watching. Marcus Bradfield's wife, for one. Valerie Bradfield had her head cocked at the best angle to overhear. Carol knew for a fact Valerie detested her mother. "So, will it be okay if I call you Mum, then?"

Roxanne wasn't about to accept that. "You don't deserve me." Her voice throbbed with lack of gratitude. "You don't deserve any of this!" Roxanne made a sweeping gesture with her arm.

"Watch it, Mum," Carol warned. "You might knock another Chinese vase off its stand. From here on in, all breakages must be paid for."

Roxanne was in no mood for humour. "To think you can joke on a day like this!"

"Make a fuss, Mum, and I'll have someone see you and Jeff out," Carol returned quietly.

"You learn fast, don't you?" Roxanne spoke with great bitterness. "You're going to be just like…"

"Get a handle on it, Mum. Damon Hunter is coming this way."

Roxanne stared halfway across the drawing room. No trouble spotting the tall, very handsome young man dressed in an impeccable dark suit. There was a man who captured attention. In photographs he looked very dashing. In the flesh he looked like a Renaissance prince with his glossy sable hair, bronze skin and brilliant coal-black eyes. "He's not going to be able to do everything for you, Carol. You'll need someone. You'll need *me*. Just remember that."

"Don't forget to remind me to remember that," Carol said drolly.

"There you go again with your wisecracks."

"I don't want to go near chucking you out, Mum. I hope you noted the big hug Jeff gave me. One of the reasons I moved out."

"God forgive you," Roxanne said, a pious look on her face. "Jeff has been a splendid stepfather to you."

"Get the blinkers off for once in your life, Mum."

As Damon approached, Roxanne's outraged face settled into an alluring smile. Roxanne was man bait. A brunette with a magnolia skin and ice-blue eyes, she looked wonderful in black.

"Introduce me," she managed, out of the side of her mouth. "I have a hundred questions to ask him."

"Just be sure you have nothing to hide."

"All families have something to hide, Carol," Roxanne answered with a brief laugh.

"Indeed they do. Especially the Chancellors. Don't expect Damon to answer any of your questions. You might have to make do with the introduction."

When it was time to leave her uncle drew her into his arms. It wasn't a close hug like Jeff's, but outwardly the action of a fond uncle. Carol experienced the same odd feeling of trepidation. Had her uncle frightened her when she was a child? If he had, she retained no memory of it. He wouldn't have dared in any case. She had been her grandfather's little princess.

"Call me when you want to take a run out to Beaumont," he said as though nothing had changed. "I can't come to grips with the fact my father left the estate to you, Carol. But I don't want you to think I blame you in any way. It was my father's idea of revenge."

"That may not have been his motive at all, Uncle Maurice. I'm my father's daughter. Grandfather's feelings of remorse must have gone very deep. I know how much you love Beaumont. You will have plenty of time to find yourself another country retreat. I believe Mayfield is coming on the market?"

Maurice Chancellor's blue eyes blazed. "My dear, I couldn't settle anywhere else other than what has been the family home. But I do want to thank you for your consideration."

"Perfectly all right, Uncle. It doesn't seem appropriate today to mention *I* got none."

That was not well received.

She sailed through her second-year exams, her personal best. She'd put in a lot of hard work. She didn't have any distractions, nor did she allow them. It would have been impossible for her to remain in the flat, even if there had been room with Tracey moving in. But from the very day her grandfather's death had hit the headlines she'd known she was about to become a target. Even then she hadn't fully realised just how bad it was to become until the memorial service given for her grandfather. Anyone who was anyone had been invited. The cathedral had been packed.

Damon had stayed close to her. Even then he had organised security to shield her, big men in dark suits. The media had been out in force, all the channels, the newspapers, the whole nine yards. They hadn't hesitated to chase her and poke microphones in her face. Even then she had felt besieged, hedged in on all sides. It was a kind of violation to have so many eyes on her. She'd got a taste of how difficult it must be for celebrities to cope with all the unwanted attention.

Damon continued to come to her rescue. He released immediate funds for her to buy a harbour-side apartment that guaranteed security. He had actually taken the time to go with her while she made a choice between three apartments that offered all she wanted. She had an idea security was still around but she never caught sight of anyone. Obviously they were professionals.

She was getting very used to Damon. *Too* used. He was becoming so familiar to her, changing her existence. His manner was always correct. One of the reasons she had worked so hard to get top marks for her end-of-year exams was that she wanted to impress Damon. Winning his approval had fuelled her efforts. Privately she acknowledged that. On a couple of occasions, she had even picked his brains. She'd told Professor Deakin, and he'd laughed. The professor was mightily pleased with her. Her tutors were equally pleased.

Damon had made a point of seeing her each week. A "catch up," he called it. Sometimes they managed coffee. Nothing like a date. Gosh, no; nothing like. She thought she could never close the gap between them. He was charming, committed, immensely helpful but clearly she was his client. His most important client, as it happened, but a line in the sand had been drawn. In any case, rifling through glossy magazines she had seen photographs of him at this or that function, always with a glamour girl on his arm.

She couldn't believe he could get serious about Amber Coleman. She might look terrific, but from all accounts she was a bird brain. Maybe the gossips were wrong. Maybe she was highly intellectual and hiding it. Didn't someone clever say it benefited the wise man to appear a fool? Sounded a bit like Confucius. Women had a long history of hiding their intelligence from men. Modern woman had a chance to totally reverse that. Why not take it? Some were very slow.

This evening was a special occasion. Damon was taking her out to a celebration dinner at arguably the best restaurant in town, and there were plenty of them to vie for top place. She had never been there. It wasn't a restaurant that catered for potentially noisy students; they had their own haunts. She continued to see her friends. She continued to help out, reminding herself not to overdo it. Especially with Amanda, who had started to act as if now she was megarich she had an obligation to look after them. She hadn't in the least minded paying for Emma's nose job. With the tip docked and the bridge reshaped, Emma was a new woman. It was heart-warming to see Em's self-confidence notch up several degrees. There was no reason why she couldn't find her prince.

She knew she couldn't wear one of her exuberant sparkly little numbers that showed off her limbs, especially her legs. She wanted to look older, more mature. She knew she couldn't look like his usual glamour girls, nor match their height. Not one of them was petite, but then he was so tall. He didn't favour short girls. Hence the killer heels, fuchsia strappy sandals to match her dress. She'd had her unruly hair cut by the best, the thickness layered to frame her face. She and the hairdresser had settled on just short of shoulder-length. It was then long enough to pull back when she wanted.

She didn't have jewellery to speak of. Well, not yet. Her mother had tons, but hadn't offered to lend her anything.

For God's sake, Carol, can't you buy something for yourself?

Her mother had barely been able to cope with her daughter's good fortune.

They'll hate you more than ever, Carol. I'd definitely keep my eye on them. They could even try to have you killed.

She hadn't been proud of her response, but her mother's warning had held more than a lick of personal satisfaction. "Well, *you'd* know all about that, Mother." If she'd delivered that crack in person, she would probably have had to have her jaw wired.

In the end she sought the advice of a very smart woman she knew, mother of one of her university friends, a lovely, kind lady. Together they had gone to a very fashionable boutique after hours where Carol had tried on various evening and dinner dresses suitable for her age and petite figure. She wanted something she could wear with ease. The last thing she wanted was to feel self-conscious. Finally, heads together, they had settled on a beautifully cut, unembellished fuchsia silk satin. It was one-shouldered, with wide ribbonlike detailing on the shouldered side. The dress hugged her figure, but it wasn't too tight. She hated that look.

"Very chic!" was the judgement.

Clearly the boutique owner had expected her to buy more and hopefully become a future customer. She intended to, so they had not embarked on a spending spree but a collection of clothes she would need. Afterwards she had rung Sydney's most admired florist to organise one of her prized baskets of exquisite summer blooms to be delivered to her mentor's address.__

The neckline didn't call for a necklace, but she definitely needed earrings. She had a pair of gold-plated drop earrings that looked like sapphires and diamonds but were actually fine cubic zirconias and dark-blue topaz. They would do. Amanda's verdict when she had first worn them: *'a trotting horse wouldn't notice the difference.'*

That had to be one of Amanda's grandmother's sayings. Amanda often quoted her maternal grandmother's pearls of wisdom. Her grandmother had been born in Ireland, something Amanda was very proud of.

How quickly did life change? Since her abandonment at age five, she had wanted to feel secure. Something else that was very important to her was trust and a feeling of companionship with a man. She had never achieved that since the days of her father and grandfather. Damon Hunter ticked all the boxes. She felt he was her loyal friend, not just her legal advisor and trustee. Her feelings ran the whole gamut of emotions. He was her friend, but never *lover*. She caught her breath at the very thought. She even dreamed about him. Dreams that ran on and on. She didn't fool herself. She had a mega-crush on him. Who could blame her? It was making it difficult for her usual beaux to get a look in.

If Carol had been at all prone to stage fright, she would have been petrified the moment they entered the restaurant. As the maître d' showed them to their table, interest was palpable. As they passed by, diners looked up to smile; some called "hello." Now and again a woman caught Damon's hand to murmur a few words Carol couldn't catch. A few heads craned to see who Damon Hunter was with. The expressions were uniformly pleasant; maybe a couple denoted envy. She was out and about with Damon Hunter, even if she was the Chancellor heiress. Carol had the idea she would never be forgiven if somehow she managed to capture his romantic attention. They need not fear. This was her reward for working hard.

"I might as well be wearing a party hat," Carol remarked when they were seated and the drinks waiter had hurried away to find Damon's choice of champagne.

"You have to get used to it, Carol. You're always going to be the centre of attention."

"That's funny! I thought they were all looking at *you*. Especially the women. Any girlfriends among the ranks?"

"Yes, possibly, a few," he acknowledged with a faint smile. "You look *exquisite!*" That was a real slip, but he was still reeling from the shock of seeing her as she'd opened her apartment door. The impact had hit him squarely in the chest, the area of the heart. He'd already known she was ravishingly pretty, but even that fell a long way short of an adequate description. She was lovely with tremendous allure and a new level of maturity. His involuntary—God help him, *passionate*—reaction was, this was a young woman he could easily fall in love with; a very sexy, sensual young woman in her beautiful plum-coloured dress with her ruby hair cut much shorter to frame her small vivid face. Girl into woman.

Only, falling in love with her was a danger to be avoided at all costs. He hadn't even dared to kiss her on the cheek. He couldn't afford to indulge in anything like that. It could turn out to be the thin edge of the wedge. But her arm just above the elbow as he had taken it as they'd moved off was so smooth to his touch. She had beautiful skin. Beautiful skin all over her body, he just knew. If for a moment he had allowed himself to be pierced by an unnerving desire, he was over it. Well…almost over it, back in control. The very last thing he wanted was to bring trouble down on Carol Chancellor's young head.

Damon sat back, his eyes hooded. If he were honest, he

would admit he didn't really know what was happening in his life any more.

He had already told her she looked beautiful the moment he had arrived to pick her up. She wasn't expecting *exquisite*. Carol took a deep breath, aware of the heat in her cheeks. "I'm glad you think so. Do I look older?"

Damon couldn't help laughing. "Was that your intention?"

"You may have noticed I'm not wearing one of my sparkly little numbers," she leaned forward to confide. "I wanted to appear more elegant." *For* you.

"You have my verdict." There was a faintly sardonic twist to his handsome mouth.

She studied him with her bluer-than-blue eyes. "What do they say, amorous intrigue is the spice of life? Do you agree?"

"You're saying this is an amorous occasion?" He quirked a brow.

He looked so attractive she felt her heart give a great lunge. "Don't be silly, Damon. You're embarrassing me. I'm talking about *your* lady friends. We can talk about them, can't we? I happen to know you've checked out my list of on-and-off boyfriends."

"Now, how would you know that?" His gaze sharpened.

"Gotcha!"

"Okay." He held out his palms. "My job is to protect you, Carol. Protect you and your interests. I have to keep one move ahead of the game. You're well and truly in the limelight. But you know you have a management team in place."

"So how long is this management team going to be in place?" She made an attempt at lightness when just being with him engendered such excitement.

The expression on his face was serious. "As long as it takes. Now, this is a celebratory dinner. You've done us all proud. What are you going to have? The seafood is always superb."

"I know. They sing paeans of praise for the chef. Thank you for thinking of me, Damon. We're friends, aren't we?"

His brilliant dark gaze held hers. "We are, Carol." Momentarily he allowed himself to barely touch her small pretty hand lying on the table. Was it an excuse? Sensation stunned him, catching him under the ribs. It set off a surge of adrenaline that ran like shivery pins and needles up and down his arm.

"That's all I need to know." Carol, too, felt the impact. For half a second she felt her heart actually flutter. She had never thought of herself as needy, yet it was thrilling to know she had Damon on her side; Damon to stand at her shoulder. He had done that from their very first meeting. She might be a client but she had the unstoppable feeling she was a little bit important to him.

The champagne arrived. He raised his glass to her. "Congratulations, Carol."

After that, they both fell into their comfort zone. If she wanted so much more, at least she had the sense to know it was out of the question. Damon was kind, he was thoughtful, he was way out of her league. She almost wished herself five or six years older. But that was her nature: she always did rush at things. She had rushed into a huge crush. One could wait all one's life for such a crush.

It was easy enough to savour the beautiful food and wine. Carol stuck to two glasses of champagne as her limit. She thought Damon would approve. At any rate, he didn't attempt to press any more on her. They talked about many things—always something fresh to discuss. He told her how he had been hell-bent on a legal career. He talked about his mother. Clearly they shared a close, loving relationship. Damon had travelled widely, sometimes to very distant places like the North Pole.

"I went with a university friend, Zac Murray. We both

wanted to have the experience of seeing the Northern Lights, the aurora borealis."

"And did you? I'd read it's not always possible, depending on the weather."

His dark eyes lit up. "We were fortunate to be there in the intense phase of the solar cycle. We lay on our backs for an hour or more, staring up at a phenomenal display. It got too cold to stay. The aurora appeared in curtainlike structures, the most marvellous fluorescent green, very bright. I have seen the aurora australis in the South Island of New Zealand when I was on holidays some years back. It had red and blue lights. Not a lot of people know the Northern Lights and the Southern Lights have almost identical features."

"In the Middle Ages the aurora was believed to be a sign from God," Carol remembered. She was an avid reader, unlike her friends, who had enough with their text books and the internet.

One side of his firm mouth lifted slightly. "Difficult to deny the existence of a divine being when confronted by the marvels of nature."

"A religious experience?

"I'm going to say a spiritual one, Carol," he said calmly.

He was focusing on her face. Was he really seeing *her* or just a pretty girl? "Maybe that's how God reveals himself," Carol suggested.

"Okay," he smiled. "I'll go along with that."

They finished the entrée of the day, blue swimmer crab with strips of smoked eggplant. It was superb, as was the steamed red emperor served in a banana leaf with papaya chilli and coconut salsa. Australian chefs were among the best in the world, she decided. Australian fresh produce was amazing. They were working their way through what they would have for dessert when a tall, very glamorous brunette rose from her seat across the room and began to wind her way towards them, stopping here and there for short two- or three-way conversations.

Carol revved into life. "How do you feel about introducing me to your girlfriend?" she asked mischievously.

He looked up, his expression half amused, half sardonic. "Which one?"

"The one coming this way. A real glamour girl. Some angst, I'd say, though it's not all that visible. Why *is* that?"

"I don't have a clue." Nevertheless he rose suavely to his feet as Amber Coleman arrived at their table. "Good evening, Amber."

"Good evening, darling." She followed up by raising her bare arms to him in a public show of closeness, then she kissed him on both cheeks. She was wearing a short strapless gown in tomato red that set off her brunette colouring beautifully. "Thought I spotted you out of the corner of my eye. And this is young Carol Chancellor?" She turned to give Carol a dazzling smile. At the same time, she made a swift judgement on Carol's appearance, make-up, hairdo, and dress, even taking a peep at Carol's stilettos.

Carol returned smile for smile. "How nice to meet you, Ms Coleman. I have a birthday in August. I'll be twenty-one."

"A marvellous age!" Amber enthused. "And this is a fabulous dinner date." She spoke archly. It didn't fool Carol for a minute. Amber Coleman was *furious*.

"Yes, and it's nearly over." Carol gave a deep sigh of regret. "I have to be in bed by nine." She glanced at her watch. "Oops, Damon, we won't be home on time."

For a split second Amber Coleman's fixed smile faded, but she quickly re-found her habitual poise. "Just wanted to say hello. You're coming to the Burtons' tomorrow night, Damon?" She shifted her golden-brown gaze back to him.

A line appeared between his black brows. "I don't know that I got an invitation, Amber."

"You *did,* darling," she said. "Oh, well…" Another glance flicked over Carol. "I suppose you're very busy."

"He is, too. I worry about him," Carol piped up with concern. "But you mustn't blame me, Ms Coleman. Damon has plenty of other important clients."

"Now that was naughty," Damon said after Amber just short of flounced away.

"Kids are allowed to be naughty. I *am* naughty, make no mistake. I'm on my best behaviour with you, Damon. I can't promise it will last. I *was* a naughty kid. It happens when family abandons you."

"You had your mother."

That earned him an enigmatic smile. "So I did. Tell me, are you going to the Burtons' knees-up?" She widened her eyes. "Did you hear what Ms Coleman said? You were invited."

Damon knew she was trying to rattle his cage. He concentrated his attention on the menu. "I'm debating the six little macaroons of different flavours or the Turkish-coffee petits pots?"

She was instantly diverted. "Why not both, then we can share? Macaroons sound easy but they're actually quite difficult to get perfect." She spoke seriously.

"You cook?" One brow lifted.

"Why look so surprised?" Her gaze was challenging.

He gave a near-Gallic shrug. "Well…"

"I know. You thought I'd be useless in the kitchen. Well, I have to tell you I'm a good cook. I devour cookbooks. I love cooking programmes. I love that French guy. I make a *wicked* chocolate-truffle tart. I used to do most of the cooking at the flat. My girlfriends were happy to leave it to me. Jeff used to love my cheesecake. My mother never touched sweets—the figure, you know? Needless to say, she never cooked. They dine out just about every night. Roxanne is actually anorexic, which is worrying. She pushes food round and round her plate. It's something to see."

"It would be," he agreed, glad she had concerns about her mother's health no matter their difficult relationship. "How do you get on with your stepfather?" He made a searching assessment of her expression.

Her eyes shot to his face. "Oh, hey, I don't talk about Jeff, Damon. Not even with you."

His handsome features tautened. "He never laid a finger on you? I saw the two of you together at the house, remember?"

"Is *that* why you charged over?" She let out a gasp. "You thought I was frightened?"

"Not frightened—you were surrounded by people—but he had his arms wrapped right around you. You're small."

Carol sat back. "Gosh, I'm glad you didn't say *short*. You gave Jeff quite a fright."

"I meant to." His disapproval of Jeff Emmett was evident. "Now here comes the waiter. I just hope the macaroons are as good as yours."

Carol laughed in delight. He had thought she was scared. His reaction had been immediate. "Maybe you should tell the chef he has plenty of competition out here."

They walked companionably to the entrance of her apartment building. Damon intended to see her right to her door. One of the wealthiest women in the city had been the recent focus of attention for a male stalker who had turned out to be an ex-groundsman at her country retreat. He had even been admitted to her building dressed as a maintenance man.

"You don't have to come up, Damon," she said

"I will, all the same." No one was loitering in the street. No one was watching from a parked car. He hated the fact that she was now a target as the Chancellor heiress. It wouldn't be possible to miss her, with her ruby-red hair, porcelain skin and the graceful ballerina's body. She had told him she had studied ballet from age six to sixteen.

"Somewhere for my mother to dump me. It just so happened I *loved* it. How did I get in this position, Damon?" she asked.

He took her elbow. "Your grandfather obviously thought you could handle it."

"With a lot of help."

"You've got it, Carol." Damon pressed the buttons for both lifts.

"But—"

"No buts. I'll see you to your door."

After a moment one lift door opened, but as they went to step in a tall, gangly young man around nineteen or twenty— jeans, blue T-shirt, shock of blond hair—charged from the back of the lift, mobile glued to his ear. He looked angry and upset, red in the face.

"Watch it!" Carol gasped. He had headed right for her, preoccupied, fair head down.

"Sorry, babe, an emergency." He glanced up. He had taken the short cut between Carol and Damon, not intending to but clipping Carol's arm and shoulder rather hard. She staggered on her high heels and Damon caught her, slipping a strong arm around her waist. She gave a convulsive swallow, her whole body suddenly pulsing with sensation. It was an extraordinary feeling to be held close to his body—no day dreaming, the real thing—her body pressed against his. She could only stand perfectly still taking little in and out breaths through her open mouth. Her flesh seemed to be burning through the silk satin of her dress. Her legs had lost so much of their strength she felt she just might slide to her knees. Only he held her. How crazy to think it, but she had a feeling she had come home! She wanted to stay there forever.

The sheer folly of it!

Damon also had a good grip on the tearaway. "Are you going to apologize for that?" he rasped.

"What the hell? You're holding me up, man. Don't start, right?" The young man took a good look at Damon, then decided on the spot to ditch all bravado. The demand eased off into a plea.

"I'll do more than that." Damon released Carol so he could get a better grip on the agitated young man.

"Look, I'm sorry, man. I didn't hurt her."

"I need you to say that to *her*. What's your name?"

The young man gave Carol a look that suddenly sparked with interest. He made a whistling sound. "Ooh, *call me pretty!* You're our very own little heiress. Aren't you—you know?—Carol Chancellor?"

"Apparently." With her own age groups, Carol was immensely sure of herself.

But Damon felt a rush of anger. "What are you doing here? Fill me in. I'm ready enough to call the police."

The young man tore his eyes away from Carol. "You've gotta be jokin' man?"

"Try me." Damon snapped.

"Look, my dad and his girlfriend live here, okay? Understand that upsets me. He's Steve Prescott. You know, the developer? He makes tons of money. I can give you some, if you like. I'm Gary."

"Don't much like your manners, Gary."

Suddenly Carol recognized the young man. "It's all right, Damon. I've seen Gary before. His father has one of the penthouses."

Gary's expression brightened. He offered his hand to Carol. "Pleased to meet you."

Carol consented to having her hand shaken. "How do you do?"

"You're even prettier than your photographs."

"How nice of you to say that."

"No problem." He turned to Damon. "Now you know who I am, can I go? I have to check in at home. I had to deliver a parcel from Mum to dear old Dad. I hope it blows up in his face."

No good feelings there, Carol thought.

"Take it slow, Gary," Damon advised. "You can get into trouble making statements like that."

"So he hurts Mum and he doesn't get hurt, is that it?"

Carol spoke up. She knew all about dysfunctional families. "Give it time, Gary. I guarantee your parents' separation won't last long."

Gary looked down at her in amazement. "You reckon?"

Carol had seen the girlfriend at least a dozen times: an airhead and a gold-digger. "That's my opinion. Trust a woman's instinct."

"You don't have to sell that to me," Gary said fervently. "Mum was the *first,* not the last, to know Dad had started playing around. Look, how about we have coffee sometime?" he suggested. "Get better acquainted. I'm surprised I haven't run into you before now."

"Literally."

"Ouch! I've moved back in with Mum. We're in the book." He named an exclusive street and a suburb.

"I'll think about it," Carol said.

"Great! I'd really like that. Can I go now, boss?" He shot a look at the tall, looming Damon.

"This time you walk away," Damon only half joked.

At her door Damon asked, "Want me to look around? It will only take a minute."

She stared up at him, suddenly all breathlessness. "You know I'm safe, Damon."

Yet it seemed to him she had lost a little colour. He

shouldn't have done it, but he couldn't help himself. You could call him a victim of her beautiful blue eyes. Just looking into them was like diving into a crystal-clear lagoon. He drew a finger a little way down her satin-smooth cheek. "I'm here. Might as well." Unnerved by his own susceptibility. he made his tone brisk. Briskness wasn't easy to project when he felt anything but.

"O—kay." The word was slowed by the flickers of excitement that raced through Carol at the rate of knots. She could heat the pulse of her heart. All because he had very lightly stroked her skin. This was *insane*. She felt shame. She didn't want him to see her excitement. She hated the very thought of making a fool of herself. She'd die if she embarrassed him. She had so much poise, so much self-confidence with the boys she knew. Damon was something else again. She was so aware of him, it was right to feel fear.

She stood motionless in the living room while Damon made a quick check. He even checked over the rear balcony.

"All clear. You feel safe here, don't you, Carol?" His dark eyes found hers.

She could have said, *I feel safe with you around,* instead she said, "Safe as a girl can be. We've all been a bit unnerved by Anne Nesbitt's stalker getting into her very secure apartment building."

Damon nodded. "Well, he's been caught." A slight pause. "Don't have coffee with the Prescott boy. Don't encourage him." He said it as though the thought worried him.

"What's this, Damon?" She was glad of the opportunity to offer a light taunt. "You're telling me what I can and can't do?"

"No, never that. But whatever you do, just be careful. There will be plenty out to exploit any weakness they could find in you. You know that." She was an extremely bright and capable, but so *young*. "I don't want you to get into the middle of the Prescott family's split-up. I happen to know it's been messy. Why did you tell Gary his father's straying might be short-lived?"

Carol shrugged. "Just a gut feeling. I've seen Steven Prescott's girlfriend. Queen of the sexpots, probably wondrously brainless. Might take him a while, but I've been told he's nobody's fool."

"Middle-age crisis," Damon said. "Men don't like to feel they're getting old, older, whatever."

"Would you cheat on your wife, Damon?"

He gave her a long look, before answering slowly. "I need to get myself a wife first, Carol. But I like to think I'm a man who would honour his wife and his vows."

"And you haven't found the right woman?" My God, what rapture for the right woman.

Was it her imagination or was there an odd stillness in the air? "Would you like to know I've found a possibility?" His dark gaze was quite unreadable.

"Not Amber Coleman, I hope?" That escaped her.

"Now now, Carol." There was a sardonic glint in his brilliant eyes.

She bit her bottom lip. "Sorry. I should have backed off."

"Amber and I are friends. Anyway, I'm in no rush to get married."

"She is." God, her tongue really was running away from her.

He walked to the door, an absolutely *beautiful* man. "I must go. I really enjoyed this evening, Carol. I hope you did, too."

She followed him up, feeling doll-like in the presence of his height. "You know I did. Thank you so much, Damon."

"It was my pleasure." He dipped his dark head and very quickly kissed her cheek. "Good night now. I'll ring you when I've gone through all your grandfather's papers. He's laid everything out on the line for you. Lew Hoffman wants to meet with you—your grandfather trusted him implicitly. He's the new chairman and CEO, as you know. Lew's a good man, very highly regarded. When you turn twenty-one you should take your place on the various boards. Marion Ellory is looking after the arts foundation. You will have to meet with her—no hurry. She knows what she's about."

"I have so much to learn."

"Happily, you've got a first-class brain. You're well informed and you have good instincts. That's a lot, I'd say."

Just a compliment, but it made her heart sing. "I want the Chancellor fortune used, Damon. I want to change people's lives. I would like to add to my grandfather's charitable foundations."

He noted the seriousness of her expression. "I see no problem with that. You really do want to be part of it, don't you?"

"I'm certainly not going to sit back and lead a useless life," she told him. "My grandfather obviously expected me to shoulder responsibility. My father would have stepped into my grandfather's shoes. Now, there's only me. I must be like my father because I'm not in the least like my mother. She lives for the social world, the right functions, the right parties."

He gave a slight grimace. "You'll have to give the right parties along the way, Carol. You won't be able to avoid it or live a *normal* life. You're young, beautiful, clever, very rich. Formidable assets. Some people would say you've got it all."

"Not *me*," Carol said and meant it. "I'd like to lead a normal life. Then there's the sad fact too much money does bad things to people and their lives. You know all about my family. Their dark side. How they treated me. God knows what they have in store for me. Troy has left messages for me. I don't answer."

"What exactly is he up to?" Damon heard himself asking too sharply.

"*He* knows. I don't. I might not have acted that way but I was shocked when he tried to come on to me. He's my cousin, for pity's sake."

"If he bothers you, you know where I am."

"I think I can handle it, Damon. You're doing enough already. I intend to keep my feet firmly on the ground. You have to trust me. I trust you. The giving and taking of it is important to me."

His eyes involuntarily moved to her lovely mouth. He couldn't look too long. His gaze shifted. "To me, too. That's what I wanted to hear, Carol. Sleep tight. I'll be in touch. If you have concerns about anything—any doubts, any fears—ring me. It doesn't matter what time."

"What if it's inconvenient?" she asked and gave a little laugh. She was loath to think of him in bed with some beautiful girl.

"Then, too," he said.

CHAPTER FOUR

THE RUN UP to Christmas was hectic. She had long talks with all of her key people, almost family style, with everyone gathered around a conference table and coffee, sandwiches and Danish pastries were brought to them. Just as she had studied hard to get good results with her end-of-year exams, she now turned her attention to finding out as much as she could about The Chancellor Group and the several foundations her grandfather had caused to be set up. Her grandfather had been bred to big business. Her father and Uncle Maurice, as well. She had not. She did, however, have a good business brain, even better than she had supposed. Enough to impress her mentors, anyway. She really wanted to be effective. She had been given duties, big responsibilities, even if she had to remind herself of that from time to time when she was force-feeding herself a wealth of information that threatened to choke her.

Her task was *huge,* but it was a great comfort to her to know she had a powerhouse of support.

To take a little pressure off her and offer some benefits, Damon suggested she might like to visit the gym where he worked out. The owner, an ex-heavyweight boxer, Bill Keegan, was a friend. He would look after her.

"He's a great guy."

"I've heard of him," Carol said. Jeff had been a big boxing fan. "You can't be expecting me to lay into him?" she joked.

Damon's answer was serious and to the point. "I believe every woman should be taught basic rules of self-defence, Carol." It was a dangerous world out there. He didn't stress that. But Carol, in her current position with so much media attention, could find herself a target for some loose cannon or someone seeking to snatch her bag. All right, she had security. He had seen to that. But he knew she found a bodyguard irksome. She was naturally adventurous. She could take risks. She had already, he had been advised, which was not unexpected. She didn't need to know how to throw punches. But naturally light on her feet, she could learn how to score points, allow herself enough time for flight.

At first Carol didn't know what to make of Damon's suggestion. She didn't think she would have much chance against just about any male. Men used their physical superiority to threaten and terrorise. Her friend Tracey had had plenty of experience of that. Tarik thankfully was out of the picture. A bit of a surprise there; Trace could be sadly weak.

Damon had taken her along to meet his friend, Bill Keegan, who had greeted her with a big smile.

"Don't you laugh at me," she said as he took in her size and weight, his bushy eyebrows raised.

"Would I dare?" He threw up huge hands. "Look, Ms Chancellor—"

"Carol, please."

"I can help you, Carol," he replied. "I can even show you how to throw a man. It's not as hard as it sounds. Damon here is my friend. He's a damned good boxer. No one as yet has managed to break his nose. I can show you easy moves at first. Then, if you stay focused, we can move on. You're small, but you can still be an effective opponent. More women should come to me, then they wouldn't be so vulnerable."

His expression lightened. "Had a little lady come to me not so long back! Her husband used to pound her when he felt like it. Eventually she decided she had to learn to fight back. They've since split up, I'm happy to say. That was after she managed to inflict certain damage, all swingin' elbows and fists and a good solid knee." He laughed, well pleased.

In the end, she stayed well over an hour, talking to Bill, who had a fund of funny stories, while observing Damon going through his paces out of the corner of her eye. Stripped to a navy singlet and navy boxing shorts, he looked jaw-droppingly virile, his bronze skin gilded with sweat from the heat of his workout.

After that, she found herself looking forward to her twice-a-week sessions, fitting her timetable to Damon's. Damon and Bill were right. She did feel more confident about handling herself, should she ever come under attack. She knew the communal car park in the basement of her building was as secure as could be, with lots of light and security cameras. But there were blind spots. She always cast her eye over the car park as she entered it, checking who was about. Car parks weren't the best places.

Gary Prescott had left some twenty-odd notes in her mail box. They all asked the same thing: Would she have coffee with him? The first note assured her he was harmless. Note ten informed her his father's girlfriend had moved out. Carol had thought she might have. She hadn't seen her around and Prescott's girlfriend had been hard to miss. Gary went on to tell her his father hadn't returned home but he was hopeful his parents could work it out. His dad wasn't really a bad guy. Married guys got into trouble all the time.

So did that mean a wife or girlfriend should expect it? Carol pondered. Some men thought little of casual sex, but Steve Prescott had installed his then-girlfriend in his luxurious penthouse. Not casual at all. Maybe Steve Prescott would change. Maybe he wouldn't. She didn't think she would like to put Gary's father to the test.

Gary Prescott wasn't the only one to suggest they meet up for coffee, though a lot of her former friends, sadly, backed off. It was as though in becoming the Chancellor heiress she existed on a different planet. Carol was determined not to change. There was harm in losing track of normal life.

"So how did you get hold of my phone number, Amber?" Carol asked when she picked up the phone and Amber Coleman identified herself. Her phone wasn't in the book. It was an unlisted number.

"Why, Damon, of course," Amber replied as though Carol was asking a silly question. "He knows he can trust me. You, too, Carol. I'd like to be your friend. I know you're several years younger, but I'm sure we'll have lots in common. You could always come to me if you needed advice—perhaps with your clothes, what to wear to what function, that sort of thing. A little bird told me you bought that lovely fuchsia gown you were wearing when Damon rewarded you with a celebratory dinner at Laura G. She has fabulous things."

Didn't people love to gossip? Gossip she could handle. But it upset her greatly to know Damon had given his on-and-off girlfriend her unlisted phone number. To add to it, he must have accounted to Amber for their dinner date as a reward for her scholarship.

Even gods have feet of clay.

She had no real knowledge of Damon Hunter. Certainly no intimate knowledge of him. Maybe falling in love made one stupid, blind to the object of one's desire? Obviously she needed a few more years on her, a few more years of very necessary experience before she took on the love game. Suddenly she was beset by doubts and suspicions. She thought that might now be a given in her new life.

Amber Coleman had called to make a coffee date. From her manner, she had every expectation of Carol's agreeing on a day soon. Damon's betrayal hit hard. Not that she would have allowed Amber Coleman into her world. She knew they would have little in common.

Except Damon Hunter.

Carol declined, citing numerous appointments. Amber didn't take that well. She couldn't hide the pique. "You must have some free time. I checked with Damon."

Is she trying to wind you up?

"Damon isn't in charge of my appointment book, Amber. In fact, I have an appointment this morning. I mustn't be late for it. Thank you for thinking of me, Amber. I'd like to know the name of your little bird. If it was Laura G, she won't be seeing me again."

Amber broke into a lavish denial. "No, no, no, *never* Laura, although one can always tell what comes out of her boutique. She has exquisite taste. Damon is my main man. He tells me everything. We're very close, as you know."

"No, I didn't know, Amber. Thank you for telling me. Obviously I'm going to have a word with Damon about being so indiscreet, even with his closest lady friends."

Carol's brisk response was clearly unexpected. More lavish protests. "Carol, Damon is incredibly discreet, I assure you. He only shares little snippets with me. I never thought for a moment you'd *mind.*"

"Just watching my back, Amber," Carol responded. "Have a wonderful day."

She hung up, unsure what to do about this.

Bad as it was, forewarned was forearmed. Obviously she had been expecting much too much of Damon. Amber had upset her. At the same time, she had pressed home an important point—the only person she could really trust was herself. She knew lots of people would be digging into her life now. It was in her interests to put up a security wall. She could of course speak to Damon. On reflection, she thought she wouldn't. Better to wait and see what else transpired.

A few days later with Christmas almost upon them she received a call from her Uncle Maurice. He had of course asked for her phone number and got it. It was family, after all, even if the family had 'dysfunctional' stamped on it.

"You're coming down for Christmas, aren't you, my dear?" he asked in his rich cultured voice. "We all want to make up for the past. It was my father, you know, who controlled us all. When you're apportioning blame—and why wouldn't you?—you could consider that. We do so want you to come. It's your home, after all. You've been good enough to allow us to stay on. We're grateful. This Christmas won't be Christmas without you."

For whatever reason her uncle was piling it on thick. *Watch your back.*

"Are you mad?" Amanda shrieked when Carol told her. "They probably want you *dead*. Doesn't it all revert to your uncle?"

"Yes, it does."

"There you are, then," Amanda said as though offering proof positive.

"Would you like to come to Beaumont with me? Your parents are still in Scotland."

"You're serious. You *are* serious?" Amanda looked ecstatic at the thought.

"Of course I'm serious. There's tons of room and you can be the one to—"

"I know—*watch your back.* Gosh, this is great news, Caro. I know Em was getting around to asking me to join her and her family, but a visit to Beaumont! Wow!"

So that was settled. There was a time when she had

planned on asking Damon to come down for a day or two, make it sound like a fun time—bring someone with him, if he liked. *Not* Amber Coleman; she had voiced her views on Amber Coleman. Maybe another girlfriend? She had seen the glossy photographs. Now she had to withhold that invitation, though it cost her some pain-filled moments, like one of her little heart strings had snapped. Life was full of sad moments.

Better get used to it.

She was used to it. They all were.

The Chancellors weren't happy people. They didn't even pretend to be.

The minute she saw him walk into the boardroom, she wavered, half-drugged by the wave of heat in her blood. She could feel the plash in her veins. Her whole being was crying out for his attention.

Pathetic. You're pathetic, girl.

Actually, she was amazed how this had all started. Damon Hunter had changed her life.

"Carol!" He acknowledged her with his beautiful heartbreaking smile. He came around to her, bending his raven head to kiss her lightly on the cheek. They had reached that stage in a remarkably short time. So far as she observed, no one appeared to find the gesture any way out of the ordinary. She was after all only twenty years of age and her lack of height reinforced her aura of youth. Occasionally she got a "teacher's pet" feeling. There was enough evidence to support the fact her key people had all grown protective of her, male and female alike. She didn't understand that her team had come not only to like her—she was totally without any side—they admired her as well for her intelligence, her admirable goals and the amount of hard work she had to put in to halfway match them.

They had come together to discuss the development of a

huge building site only recently secured following demolition of the old building. Architects and engineers sat around the table. Since he had taken over the administration of Carol's trust, Damon had been voted onto the Chancellor Group board, a huge step up even for him. Clearly this had been Selwyn Chancellor's intention. At intervals Damon gave her a half smile across the table. One of the engineers was as good as bullying his partner into agreeing to a plan he had put forth. Finally, with the last word coming from Lew Hoffman by way of an excellent suggestion by Damon, a compromise was reached.

Carol said her goodbyes, preparing to walk to the bank of lifts, when Damon caught her up.

"Where are you off to in such a hurry?" He had felt the negative vibes, surprised and not a little thrown by them. He valued Carol's good opinion and the bond they had formed. No one could possibly question he wasn't doing his very best for her, but knew he had a lot of eyes on him. Some would be happy to break the strong lawyer-client bond. He knew he had the entire situation under control and he was one hundred per cent committed to giving his all to Carol Chancellor, his client, and Carol Chancellor, his friend. Or so he had hoped.

She tilted her face to him. No one was ever going to eclipse him, she thought drearily. "I'm so sorry, Damon, did you want me for something?"

He stared down into her softly flushed face. She was wearing a sleeveless silk dress in a shade of cobalt that made a dazzle of her eyes. "What's the matter? Clearly something is."

"An open book, am I?" Was her unexpectedly sharp reply.

"Carol, I always check to see you're okay."

"Well, I'm fine, Damon." She gave him her best smile.

It didn't fool him one bit. "A little testy, perhaps? If there's anything bothering you, you should tell me about it."

One of the lifts arrived. The door opened. He took her

elbow as they both stepped in. Damon pressed a button and the lift began its smooth, silent descent.

She'd had no intention of bringing up the reasons for her upset. But too much adrenaline was pumping through her. It blew the lid. Once started, she swiftly found she was out of control. "Why ever did you give out my phone number to Amber Coleman?"

He reacted just as fast. "Would you run that past me again?"

"Amber Coleman, your close friend," she stressed. "She rang me to arrange coffee and a chat."

"Are you serious?" His tone deepened and darkened.

"You bet I am. She might be a pal of yours, but I don't like her."

"I'm well aware of that, Carol."

"All the more reason for you not to hand out my number."

"So that's very clear to you, is it?" His dark baritone was edged with ice.

They had reached the ground floor. He kept alongside her until they were out of the building and in the busy street. There Damon drew her into the near arcade. "You're saying Amber told you she got your number from me?"

"Made a point of it." Carol was well past tiptoeing around the subject. She knew she was giving herself away showing how very upset she was but she couldn't stop now.

"And you believed her?" he asked in brusque fashion.

Our very first argument.

"Well…" She gazed up at him with accusation. "That's how it went down."

"I see." He paused for a moment, as though getting himself together. "Weren't you the one who spoke about how important mutual trust is?" he challenged.

Carol wasn't a redhead for nothing. She fired up. "Don't you attempt to lecture me, Damon."

Send For
2 FREE BOOKS
Today!

I accept your offer!

Please send me two
free Harlequin® Romance
novels and two mystery
gifts (gifts worth about $10).
I understand that these books
are completely free—even
the shipping and handling will
be paid—and I am under no
obligation to purchase anything, ever,
as explained on the back of this card.

❏ I prefer the regular-print edition
114/314 HDL FNPS

❏ I prefer the larger-print edition
119/319 HDL FNPS

Please Print

FIRST NAME

LAST NAME

ADDRESS

APT.#   CITY

STATE/PROV.   ZIP/POSTAL CODE

Visit us online at
www.ReaderService.com

Offer limited to one per household and not applicable to series that subscriber is currently receiving.

Your Privacy—The Reader Service is committed to protecting your privacy. Our Privacy Policy is available
online at www.ReaderService.com or upon request from the Reader Service. We make a portion of our mailing
list available to reputable third parties that offer products we believe may interest you. If you prefer that we not
exchange your name with third parties, or if you wish to clarify or modify your communication preferences, please
visit us at www.ReaderService.com/consumerschoice or write to us at Reader Service Preference Service, P.O. Box
9062, Buffalo, NY 14269. Include your complete name and address.

H-R-S13 ▲ Detach card and mail today. No stamp needed. ▲ © 2011 HARLEQUIN ENTERPRISES LIMITED. ® and ™ are trademarks owned and/or used by the trademark owner and/or its licensee. Printed in the U.S.A.

What do you think you're achieving, exactly? The voice of reason cut in like a blade.

He glanced at her distressed face then said quietly, "Let's walk. I'm very surprised Amber told you that."

She obeyed him. She badly needed to repair her nerves. "Are you saying it's a lie? She did it out of malice?"

"She was mistaken," Damon clipped off.

"And that's an answer?"

He took her arm. They were inside the famous Queen Victoria Building, built in 1898 to celebrate Queen Victoria's Golden Jubilee. There was a figure of the Queen surrounded by royal jewellery and costumes as well as a life-size Chinese imperial bridal carriage made of solid jade. They were about to pass one of the prestige jewellery shops in the arcade, with a glittering display in the window. Damon turned her as though they intended to study the display. Neither of them did. They had far different things on their minds.

"No, Carol, that's a *fact*." Damon spoke with utter sincerity. "I did not give Amber your phone number. I would never give out your phone number without your permission." And maybe not even then, he thought, but didn't add.

"So who told her?"

"At this point, I don't know. Amber is better than most at ferreting out information. I'll put it to her."

Carol bowed her head, abashed. "No, forget about it, Damon. I declined her offer anyway. She's busy checking me out. But you *did* tell her all about the celebratory dinner you organised for me?" She decided it would be better to withhold further revelations like where she had bought her evening dress from. It was extremely important to her to have Damon on her side. Now she thought she might have muffed it, his dark eyes were so sombre.

"Can you *really* see me doing that?"

She braced herself. "I'm sorry, Damon, but it matters to me."

"And it matters to me," he clipped off.

"Sorry, sorry." She hoped some sort of an apology would count. "I believe she wants me out of your life, Damon, for whatever reason. She wants me to stay out."

"Possibly," Damon admitted. He was well aware of Amber's jealous nature and her propensity for playing games. "I'll see to it she doesn't trouble you again."

"No, leave it, please, Damon," she said in agitation. "It's my fault. I'm too naive. I believed her. My apologies."

His eyes hadn't left her lovely upset face. "Accepted." Jealousy was in the nature of things. He had seen Amber at two functions. He hadn't partnered her on those occasions. He had gone with a female colleague, Rennie Marston, a good friend some five or six years older than himself with the grace, wit and intelligence Amber lacked. Amber wouldn't have been jealous of Rennie. In Amber's eyes Rennie would have been well and truly over the hill. But Carol Chancellor was a fresh-as-a-rosebud twenty-year-old. He thought he had kept all sexual interest in Carol well hidden. But Amber, sharp as a tack in that department, must have spotted it.

A flippant superior-styled voice came from behind them, surprising and dismaying them. "You know, the two of you look for all the world like a couple checking out engagement rings?"

Carol spun to face her cousin. She was in control again. "You're watching way too much TV, Troy. We're talking business."

"Of course." Troy bent his head. Clearly his intention was to kiss her only Carol, seeing the kiss coming, turned her face away. It wasn't good to so dislike one's cousin.

Troy was not to be put off. "Dad tells me you're coming

to Beaumont for Christmas," he continued in the same flippant vein.

"Uncle Maurice *has* gone very social," Carol remarked dryly.

"I tell you, it just gets better and better," Troy declared. "We should have a glorious time."

We? Damon didn't like this new development one little bit. It disturbed him. He had hoped there would be no secrets between them. Clearly, that wasn't the case. Carol hadn't said a word to him about spending Christmas at Beaumont. Not that she really needed to, but he had thought… Obviously he had presumed too much.

"Invite a friend if you like, Troy." Carol spoke casually, but she had seen a course of action. Jumped at it. "I've already invited a girlfriend and *Damon* will be spending a few days with us, won't you, Damon?" She smiled at him as she would a dear friend.

For an instant Troy looked more than angry. He looked slighted, even enraged.

"It's difficult for Damon, but he has promised." She pinned Damon's eyes, knowing he would save her any embarrassment by backing her.

That on-the-spot invitation presented no difficulty for Damon. As it happened, he welcomed it to the point when he had to seriously consider Carol Chancellor's importance in his life. He didn't just like and respect her. He had been afraid he was falling in love with her. Probably too true. Nevertheless, he shot back a pristine white cuff to look at his watch. "Wouldn't miss it for the world. We should be heading off, Carol."

"Heading off where?" Troy demanded to know. He just hated Damon Hunter, the crackerjack lawyer, and didn't bother to hide it. Every feature of his good-looking face was stiff with what could only be interpreted as jealousy.

"Business, business, business," Carol chanted.

"Money, money, money," Troy snorted. "But hey, don't let me stand between you and your ill-gotten gains." He had thought that in paying attention to little Carol he might be rewarded. He'd had that reward in mind for some time; was savouring it, in fact. She seemed to get more beautiful every time he saw her. She was certainly very fashionably and expensively dressed. No student-type gear any more. He bitterly resented Hunter's strong presence in her life. They were getting *way* too close.

"A legally watertight inheritance from your grandfather." Damon put him straight. "And I'd advise you not to make any slanderous statements or make an enemy of your cousin. That goes for me, too, as Carol's attorney."

It was apparent even to Troy, who had been angry all his life, that he had strayed into dangerous waters. He backed down. "Don't you think it understandable we're unhappy about what the old man did?" he whined. "My mother is right. It was revenge, pure and simple."

"Only revenge is neither pure nor simple," Damon warned. "It would be a huge mistake for you to go looking for it. You know the saying: before you embark on your journey of revenge, dig two graves."

"Bible, right?" Troy shot a glare at Damon.

"Confucius," Carol corrected with a sparkle in her eyes. "I urge you, Troy, to accept our grandfather's decision. I know you were brought up believing you're entitled to every good thing in life. As far as that goes, our grandfather left us all an indecent amount of money. I intend to use my share wisely."

Troy responded with an apology. "I didn't intend to upset you, Carol. I'm more than happy to see you back in my life. You always were a clever little thing. Now you're very, very *special*."

The long look Troy Chancellor gave his cousin was very definitely sexual.

That was most unfortunate, Damon thought, not to mention dangerous. Instinct told him Carol's cousin, Troy, could turn into a potential problem.

Damon saw her into her next port of call, her favourite department store, David Jones, although the city's central business district was a serious shopper's dream. She had run out of a few items of make-up that needed replacing. She had found these days she had to look just *so*. "Sorry if I embarrassed you back there," she said. "I don't need Troy's attention."

"Well, you have to know you've got it," Damon replied very dryly.

"That's why I said you were coming to Beaumont for a few days. I can't spend time trying to analyse Troy's various hang-ups."

"But you know he's got them?"

"I think he was born with them," Carol said as her memories of Troy the boy came creepy-crawling back.

"So I'm protection?"

"Something like that." Carol flashed him a crystalline-blue glance. She would *welcome* his acceptance!

"Hmm...!" He looked away over her radiant head. "I wondered why you didn't tell me you were spending Christmas with the Chancellors. I just can't identify that lot as your family."

"Nothing I can do about it." Carol shrugged. "I was going to tell you, Damon. But something got in the way."

"Someone, you mean?"

"Well...that. I would love you to come, Damon, but I know you will have plans."

He had. At least one had included her. Now this! "No

plan that I can't put off," he said lightly. "Or change to another time."

"Does that mean you *will* come?"

Her open pleasure was infectious. "The answer is simple. I'm here for you, Carol. What days were you thinking?"

Her spirits soaring, she started to fill him in. "I'm planning on driving there Christmas Eve. Uncle Maurice issued the invitation. He sounded very much like he wants to make amends."

There was a sudden glitter in Damon's clever dark eyes. "Did you swallow it?"

Carol winced at the dry-as-ash tone. "How could I? He spoke like he was very kindly *inviting* me to what is now my own home. It's going to be hard to evict Uncle Maurice and dear Dallas. Poppy's will smashed all their expectations to smithereens. It's going to take time for it all to sink in."

For someone so young, she displayed a bemusing maturity.

"By the way, I invited my friend from uni, Amanda Gregson. You met her briefly."

"The cheeky one?"

"That's Amanda. She's very bright, you know. I told you, she's the one who constantly tells me to watch my back with the family. She'll come down with me. I suppose you can't possibly come for Christmas Day?"

"Now, what can you offer as an enticement?" He slanted her a deliberately uncomplicated smile.

"The best Christmas dinner you've ever had." She made an on-the-spot promise, acutely aware she had blushed when there had been little or no innuendo in his tone. Why would there be? "You can bring a friend, if you like."

"Okay, I'm in, but I'll come alone. I'll drive down late afternoon. I'm bound to have a few outstanding matters to settle first."

"God bless you!" Carol couldn't help herself. She spoke

fervently. They were standing in a quiet spot against an exterior wall, but she had actually ceased to be aware of her surroundings with well-dressed shoppers hurrying to and fro. She was equally unaware they had been the intense focus of a good many people, two in particular. Apart from the fact they were so good-looking and such perfect foils, their faces had become known to the public.

"Why are you doing this, Carol?" Damon asked very seriously. "You know the lot of them are consumed with envy. Your uncle is not to be trusted."

"Some part of me knows that for certain," Carol said. "Some fragment of memory. I don't know what it is. You think he would try to hurt me?"

Damon turned his elegant hands out. "Maurice Chancellor wouldn't be fool enough to do such a thing." Chancellor would make sure he could never be accused of anything. But a man with his resources inevitably had people to do things for him. "He would never be so stupid." He had no intention of creating additional concerns for Carol, but that childhood memory of hers troubled him as much as it apparently troubled her. Was a five-year-old child's memory at all reliable? Yes, he thought, going on his own recollection of his father.

"Perhaps not." Carol sighed. "But I wouldn't put it past him to have a dogsbody always on hand to do his dirty work for him," she said, echoing his own thoughts. "The rich don't soil their hands."

She had well and truly figured her uncle out. "Don't allow your mind to run along those lines, Carol."

"Most families have family feuds, I guess," she said poignantly.

Especially the rich.

"Why are you *really* going?" Damon felt she had a definite agenda.

"I want to search the house for more photographs Poppy

might have had taken," she answered readily. "I want to find everything I can of my father's. You know, some people thought my mother deliberately left my father to drown."

"People love to talk, Carol," he said gently. "You can't stop them."

"Have you ever noticed how a lot of people born to privilege and every advantage in life die early?" She stared up into his eyes.

"A lot die *because* of it," Damon, the lawyer, said. "Drugs, an offshoot getting mixed up with the wrong people, lifestyle, high-powered cars, neuroses when things don't go exactly as they want. I know none of that applied to your father. It was an accident—accidents can and do happen frequently on boats."

"Maybe all the cruel gossip ruined my mother," Carol suggested, hanging on his answer.

"Maybe," Damon said, not believing it for one moment. He had only met Roxanne Emmett once, at Selwyn Chancellor's funeral. He had seen behind the high-gloss, sexy mask. Here was your classic narcissist, centred on *self.* He had the dismal feeling if he did a bit of research he might unearth the possibility Adam Chancellor had wanted a divorce. There was bound to have been a pre-nuptial agreement limiting what Roxanne would get should the marriage fail; Selwyn Chancellor would have seen to that. From all accounts, Roxanne Chancellor had been spoiled rotten by a husband who just could have discovered in a relatively short time a woman totally different from the one he'd thought he had married. Maybe no one would ever know what had actually happened that tragic day. But one thing was certain—Carol's father, the father who had so loved her, was long gone.

What had his dazed thoughts in his last struggling moments? Or had he been unconscious?

Only God and Roxanne Chancellor-Emmett knew.

CHAPTER FIVE

THE ART SHOWING was well under way before Damon arrived. He had promised to make an appearance as a favour to a good client. The gifted artist was her son. The showing was entitled SCAPES, Land, Sea and Air. From what he could glimpse through the crush, the paintings were very good. At least, the ones he could see.

He was making his way to his client's side—she had already spotted him and was waving him over—when he came face to face with Amber Coleman.

"Ah, the *exact* person I wanted to see!" Amber's beautifully styled dark head was held unnaturally high. Very much in the confrontational position, he thought in dismay. It was accompanied by a twisted little smile. Evidently he was supposed to feel some sort of guilt. About what? He had never made any promises to Amber. Indeed their relationship, such as it was, was open. He saw other young women. She saw other men.

Tonight she was with James Brooks, a mutual friend. James was her standby. "Flyin' high these days, Damon," she said like an accusation. "Don't see much of you at all." Here was a woman throwing down the gauntlet.

He didn't know whether to laugh or get annoyed. Instead, he glanced away, holding up a hand to James, who was fast beating a diplomatic retreat. "Amber, you know I have a pretty heavy workload. I'm only here tonight because San-dra Milton is a good client of mine."

"I *know* that," she retorted, a sharp expression on her face. "A little bird tells me you're actually having Christmas with the Chancellors." She said it with such irony Damon gave a mild groan.

"Not *another* little bird? Would this one happen to be Troy Chancellor?"

Amber couldn't frown. She'd just had another Botox in-jection. "What do you mean, *another little bird?*"

"Little birds are chirruping to you all the time, aren't they, Amber? You're a veritable magnet for information," he re-minded her.

"Oh, that!" Amber felt quick relief. It had been a constant worry that the little heiress had gone complaining to him. "People tell me things they tell no one else."

"I bet only *once,*" Damon stressed.

Amber ignored that. "Troy tells me he's concerned you're getting way too close to his cousin." She watched his expres-sion harden. Damon Hunter was a marvellously handsome man, so charismatic people just stared at him. Every day he gained more and more recognition. Being Carol Chancellor's lawyer had quite a bit to do with it, Amber thought. She had been relentless in her pursuit of Damon, but upsettingly un-successful. Any woman he took an interest in automatically became her enemy.

"Troy Chancellor would do well to watch his tongue," Damon was saying. "The rich can be very litigious."

Amber held up a hand, her long fingernails painted the same silver as her short sexy dress. "What are you saying?"

"Nothing beyond that, Amber. *You,* I'm forced to point out, have the knack of making trouble. Remember the Todds? You can be very indiscreet." Amber and her gossip had helped wreck the marriage.

Amber flushed violently. "*You* should talk! As it happens, I was with Troy when the two of us witnessed your *tête à tête* with Carol Chancellor in the QVB this afternoon." She didn't mention the sight of them staring into one another's eyes had almost given her a heart attack. She had even thought they might be looking at engagement rings.

"Look, Amber, where are you going with this?" Damon asked. "I've enjoyed your company on many occasions. I assume you have mine. But neither of us has made any commitment to the other. Far from it. Carol Chancellor is my client. I look after all my clients."

"Not like *her!*" Amber's tone was so strident, heads turned to look at her. She was oblivious, clutching Damon's jacketed arm. She squeezed hard. "You fancy her, don't you?"

Damon gently removed her hand. "My first thought is, it's none of your business, Amber. My second is, spread any misinformation and you could find yourself in trouble. Carol Chancellor is not yet twenty one."

"So what?" There was a trembling outrage in Amber's voice. "She's well and truly of marriageable age. It just so happens I know what's going to happen before it happens. Call it a woman's intuition."

"I call it paranoia. Tell me, are you dead set on a public skirmish?" Damon asked very quietly. "I think if you move off it would be eminently sensible. You're jealous, Amber. That much is clear. Just don't make quantum leaps. You've made an inordinate number of them already."

Amber retaliated by leaning into him, her voice slightly slurred. "Think your little Carol will believe me when I tell her we're long-time lovers and that you've promised me marriage?"

"You think she'll believe you before me?" Damon looked down at her, unable to hide his disgust.

"I just want to let her know not to trust you, Damon. It

would be a very easy matter for you to break her heart. She's halfway in love with you, the silly little thing. Just make sure *you* don't drown in her big blue eyes."

"Very beautiful blue eyes, I agree," he said suavely. "I'm in no danger of drowning. Thank you for your concern. Go back to James, Amber," he advised. "You're wasting your time with me."

Without mentioning it to her, Carol soon found out Uncle Maurice had invited three of his cronies with their wives, or at least two wives and the reigning girlfriend of the four-times-married Manny Bishop, a very successful, if somewhat dodgy, entrepreneur. Obviously her uncle thought he could walk right over her.

"I knew you wouldn't mind, my dear," he told her in syrupy tones, while patting her shoulder. "Plenty of room. In fact, it's good to see the house full. Maybe you would like to join us in the little shoot I've organised. All perfectly legal, my dear, in case you have concerns. Just a few quail."

Carol was aware her uncle loved to play the country squire. "I don't like guns and I don't like shooting, Uncle Maurice. I certainly have no interest in shooting quail."

"But you'd buy quail and duck from the supermarket, wouldn't you, my dear?" he parried blandly. "Urbanites like to distance themselves from the actual killing of the range of animals they eat. I assure you, I'm a clean shot. So are my friends—that's important. Nothing suffers. We have no disrespect for wildlife and we are not endangering a species. Far from it.

"You've probably eaten Mussaman curry of duck, roast duck baked with tomatoes and herbs? Wonderful dishes—so, too, is roasted stuffed quail or quail wrapped in prosciutto with ricotta, sage and chard. Yum! There is a case for shooting, you know, even game birds, which we have in abundance. The country is overrun with kangaroos, emus, wild pigs, foxes and rabbits in huge areas where they do tremendous damage. I hope you're not going to spoil a bit of sport for us? We're not going after ducks, you know. You and your friend Amanda should come along, if only for the walk, and maybe admire the marksmanship."

"And when is this to happen, Uncle Maurice?" Carol asked the moment her uncle concluded his spiel.

"Boxing Day, my dear. Around dusk, when they're on the wing to the roost. You know the origin of the term Boxing Day?"

Carol could see he was getting ready to tell her. She forestalled him. "Yes, Nona told me on one of our walks around the fountain when I was a little girl. She was the one who started the custom here of giving Christmas boxes to the staff. Well-off households traditionally gave presents or money to their loyal employees. It's a custom I want maintained. In fact, I'm glad you brought that up, Uncle Maurice. I'm assuming that will happen this Boxing Day some time well before the shoot?"

Maurice recovered quickly. "It will have to be money this year, my dear," he said smoothly, unhappy about getting rid of a stash of cash in the safe. "With father's death, no-one was of a mind to buy presents."

Carol nodded. "I dare say the staff would prefer money. I'll see you're reimbursed." Carol wanted no favours.

Damon watched the sports car come up way too fast in his rear vision. There was an eighty-kilometre speed limit on the road they were now on. The driver would know that. Signs were posted along the way. The car shot past, coming very close.

"Damned fool!"

It took Damon a second more to realise it was Troy Chancellor at the wheel. Troy Chancellor with a blonde young woman in the passenger seat. Troy Chancellor really was a bit of a clown and not to be trusted. He was the archetype of a young man ruined by money. He could even be self-destructive. He'd already demonstrated he was looking to get closer to his cousin. He didn't need money; unless he became enormously profligate, he was set up for life. No, he wanted to get close to his cousin because of the sexual excitement she engendered.

God knew what the Christmas break would bring. The truth was he had accepted Carol's invitation—apart from the scintillating pleasure he had in her company—because he wanted to protect her. Looking out for Carol Chancellor had become something of an obsession. It consumed him. The big regret was not that she was years younger than he—she was very mature for her age—but that she was an *heiress*. The Chancellor heiress. He had to admit that aspect of their relationship created a huge barrier in his mind. The last thing in the world he wanted was to be thought a man in the ideal position to take advantage of her. He had to face it, but gossip had already started. It was the way of the world. Carol was big news.

As for him, he was Carol Chancellor's lawyer, but he could be the man who had jockeyed himself into Selwyn Chancellor's good graces. He could be the man determined on winning her hand. The general thinking would be, what a coup, a gift-wrapped opportunity. Only he didn't see it that way. If Carol were a young woman he had met at some function and not Carol Chancellor the heiress, he would have been set on his course of getting to know her a whole lot better.

He had never forgotten his first sight of her. He never would.

The flash sports car that had sped past them earlier was parked in the gravelled drive by the time he arrived. He would have to avoid any confrontation with Troy Chancellor; this was Christmas, after all. He knew the very sight of him irritated Troy immensely. He was jealous, of course. Another one who followed their instincts. He supposed it was difficult to completely hide one's attraction from interested parties making a case study of the two people involved. Amber had warned him not to drown in Carol's sapphire-blue eyes. It was already too late.

Carol herself came to the door, looking grateful to see him. She didn't wait for his courteous kiss on the cheek. She stood on tip-toe to kiss him. "I'm so pleased you're here," she whispered near his ear.

"What's up? Is there a problem?"

She gave a faint shudder. "I want to put the Christmas tree up. I know we had one. I believe it was a Christmas tradition. But Dallas is totally against it. For some reason she's playing at grief. Such hypocrisy! She was in no way close to my grandfather. Do you think we should put the Christmas tree up, Damon?" She sought his opinion as though it mattered to her.

"I fail to see why not."

She looked up to give him her dazzling smile. "Okay, you have to help me. It must be stored away in the attic. But first I'll show you to your room. I'm so pleased you decided to come, Damon. I know you were obliging me."

"Not at all."

She led the way. She was wearing a white silk tank-top with a nautical navy stripe over cropped-leg navy trousers. A decorative red belt was slung around her tiny waist matching the red sandals on her feet. A simple outfit, but she looked amazingly chic.

He had no quarrel with his guest room. It was great. It was in a steel-and-glass addition to the rear of the house with unobstructed views over the beautiful landscaped grounds. It was late afternoon yet the room was bathed in golden light. White dominated the colour scheme, the only touches of colour coming from the soft greyish-blue cushions on the single armchair and the rug thrown over an armless matching sofa. Someone had placed blue hydrangeas in a glass vase on the bedside table below the tall white lamp.

"I'll be more than happy here, Carol," he said.

"You're lucky—you have an en suite." She extended an arm.

"Won't that put someone's nose out of joint?" He had to assume not all the bedrooms had an adjoining en suite. It was an old house after all, albeit a mansion.

"Oh, that doesn't matter. Their noses are out of joint already." She turned to leave. Now he could study the back of her head. She had twisted her hair into a captivating little knot, exposing her shell-like ears and her nape. Fiery little tendrils sprang out everywhere, onto her nape, her forehead, and her temples. He had the mad desire to pick her up in his arms, cradle her awhile, then lay her down gently on the bed and make endless love to her. They could fall asleep together entwined, awakening only to make love again…

Remember your role, for God's sake.

To take advantage of Carol would be morally reprehensible.

"Come down when you're ready," she was saying, snapping him out of his thoughts. "Uncle Maurice has asked some of his friends and their wives. Troy's here with his current girlfriend, Summer, who seems to have hit it off with Amanda. That's good. They can keep one another entertained while we explore the attic. What I really want to find is everything pertaining to me and my father. My mother, too, I guess. I overheard someone say only recently my grandfather's power and influence got my mother off a serious charge."

"It's a claim that has been made many times before, but

not true. It's as I told you, Carol. People love to talk. They make things up."

Her blue eyes met his. Imploringly, he thought. "What if we find something out?"

"Like what?" He frowned.

"I'm sorry I'm involving you in this. But, young as I was, I was aware my parents weren't…happy together."

"Carol, you couldn't begin to count the number of married couples who are dissatisfied with one another and their lives. They don't go around killing one another."

"I've thought of all that, Damon," she said, shaking her head. "But I can't help wondering. I wouldn't be surprised either if my mother and Jeff turn up. I couldn't reach her. I left messages. She knows I'm here. She might even know *you're* here. Your friend Amber, I've heard, is something of a troublemaker."

He couldn't deny that. "So *what* have you heard?"

His handsome face had tautened. She couldn't hold his brilliant black gaze. "Nothing much. Let's forget it. Dinner is at eight. Drinks seven-thirty. We've got plenty of time to explore the attic. After dinner you might like to help decorate the tree."

"Carol, I'll do anything you require of me," he said.

Indifferent to anyone's wishes but her own, Roxanne Emmett told her husband they would be driving out to Beaumont for Christmas.

"What!" Roxanne would never cease to amaze him.

"I said, we're heading for Beaumont. Carol is my daughter, my only child. She wouldn't dream of spending Christmas without me."

"Just how often have you dreamed of spending Christmas without her?" Jeff retaliated. "Come on, give me a break,

Roxy. They hate you out there. You're not invited. You're the woman who let Adam Chancellor drown."

"That doesn't hurt me any more, Jeff—all the heartless insinuations. I would no more have let Adam drown than you."

"Right," said Jeff. "Then I'm keepin' off boats."

Damon, as one might expect, had been greeted with enthusiasm by all the women, including Amanda and Troy's blonde girlfriend of the month, Summer Horton. She gave Damon a very thorough assessment.

Maurice Chancellor maintained his role of charming host. His three cronies, known by reputation to Damon, were pleasant. Troy gave his usual scowl. Dallas, on top form, refused point-blank to loosen up. She repeated her objection to putting up the Christmas tree but Carol politely overrode her.

"My grandfather, if he were here, would have no objection. My grandmother would have been very pleased. So the Christmas tree goes up. Damon and I are off to the attic to see where it's stored."

A friend of Maurice Chancellor offered his help to bring it down. "Is it big?"

"Very big," Dallas said, looking like she felt her late father-in-law's demise sharply.

"Fancy a walk around outside?" Amanda asked Summer. Amanda felt she was in fairyland.

"Ooh lovely!" Summer stood up, her short dress showing off her short, curvy figure. Summer had tried very hard to get Troy Chancellor's attention—making a connection with rich guys was her known objective—only Troy Chancellor was proving to be such a self-satisfied jerk!

The attic was a huge space. Damon turned on the lights while Carol paused in the doorway, peering in. To Damon's eyes she looked nervous, even a bit frightened. "What is it, Carol?"

He found himself holding out a hand, his brows knitted in concern.

"It's a scary place, isn't it?" Her soft tone faded into silence. She might have been seeing ghosts, yet she came to him, allowing him to lock her fingers in his.

He stared around them, perplexed. He had expected cluttered chaos but the extensive under-roof area, although stacked like an Aladdin's Cave with unused or unwanted treasures, was generally speaking ordered. He could see chairs, bureaux, tables, rosewood stands—Chinese by the look of them—cabinets of all kinds, bronze and marble busts of God knew who, Coromandel screens, a complete set of Louis Vuitton luggage, stacked paintings in overly ornate gilded frames, chests in abundance, wedding chests, carved chests, painted chests, you name it. Lamps of all kinds sat on tables and stands, many hung with glittering lustres. A Victorian mahogany long-case clock stood against a wall. It didn't look as though the family had thrown out a thing in the entire time they had occupied the house. There were no spooky drapes thrown over anything, no cobwebs, little sign of dust, although there would inevitably be dust. Just a mind-bending conglomeration of no-doubt valuable but disused things.

"It would be one hell of a job cataloguing all this," he said wryly.

She didn't answer. She was staring about her. Carol Chancellor was a strong young woman, but right at that moment she was on edge. Was her subconscious making some very unpleasant connections? "I haven't been up here since I was five years old," she whispered to him as though fearing being overheard.

"Who did you come with?" He suddenly wanted to put a face to that person. He hadn't forgotten that fleeting look of alarm that had passed across her face when she had first met her uncle after fifteen long years. Her face wore much the same expression right now.

"I don't know. Bit of a sad case, me."

"In what way, Carol?" He hated to see her troubled.

"We lock down on what we don't want to remember. Isn't that right?" She lifted her glowing head to him.

"We all tend to keep things we don't want to confront below the surface." He continued to hold her hand. She made no attempt to pull away. They stood together. "We lodge them at the back of our minds. What do you think happened here, Carol? What frightened you when you were a little girl?"

She shook her head, almost in desolation. "So many un-answered questions in my family, Damon. Bad blood." The strength his hand transmitted was penetrating right through her. She stared about her silently for a moment more. He didn't hurry her. "I think I remember…crawling behind one of the chests—the Italian one."

He didn't know which one that was. "Point it out."

She did.

"You couldn't have come alone. You came with someone. Or did you find your way up here by yourself? I can imagine your doing that. You would have been an adventurous child."

"Well, yes, I'm not saying I didn't get into trouble. I used to pretend Beaumont was a palace and I was the little prin-cess. It all belonged to me. Something happened here, Damon. But it won't *come*."

"No recurring dreams?"

"Many, many dreams about my father," she admitted sadly. Even with Damon beside her strange fears were crawling around in her. "But enough of that!" She looked up at him, trying for a smile. "We came to find the Christmas tree, didn't we? Not talk about *my* neuroses."

"You're no way neurotic, Carol. I believe, now you're back at Beaumont, your memory will come. We won't push it.

When you remember you must tell me. Promise?" He couldn't bear to consider the thought someone might have molested her. Anything was possible, even to those in highly privileged places.

"Oh, I will," she said with a surge of relief.

"Why don't you let me find the Christmas tree?" he suggested, drawing her forward until they were beside a set of four Louis-style armchairs with silk damask upholstery and rich gilding. They could have been genuine eighteenth century for all he knew.

"It's okay I don't want to sit down. I want to make use of our time. Why don't you find the tree and all the decorations? They would be in one of the chests. I think—" her eyes swept the space "—the bluey-green one painted with tulips. The tree obviously would be in one of the tall cupboards."

"Right!" Damon moved off. He found all the glittering baubles stored in the green chest, but it would take a little longer to find the tree. There was just so much stuff. Incredible, really. The Chancellors had been big-time hoarders.

Carol walked quickly down the centre aisle. She knew she would have to come back again over the next few days, but for now she was intent on starting her investigation. She began to open boxes. There were so many of them. She could take her pick of dozens. Writing boxes, table boxes, toiletry boxes, knife boxes, decanter boxes. She began opening others at random that might store documents. She was vaguely aware Damon had located the Christmas tree and the decorations collected over many long years.

Frustrated, she opened an old travelling trunk, then jerked back in shock. Suddenly and beyond doubt she knew why the attic held such fears for her. Her face pale, she fell to her knees, taking out a large wedding portrait and studying it.

"What have you found?" Damon came to her, alerted not only by her silence but the tension in her slight frame.

Wordlessly she held up the silver-framed photograph.

"The bride is clearly your mother. The handsome bride-groom is your father." That much was obvious. The Chancellor brothers had been very much alike.

From paleness, she flushed. "Beautiful, wasn't she? Still is. A beautiful sexy woman who didn't give a damn about doing wrong. Never repented. Never, ever!" Despite the fact she was fighting for control, Carol burst into tears.

"Carol!"

Self-consciously, she dipped her head. She didn't want Damon to see her cry, but she couldn't stop the tears. They flowed.

"Carol," Damon murmured again. His voice was quiet and, beyond that, *tender.* It was impossible not to offer comfort. He took her into his arms, the enormous surge of pleasure he felt counterbalanced by his concern. "What is it?"

She *couldn't* tell him. Much as she trusted Damon, she still had to protect her mother.

"I don't know which way is up any more," she murmured. Damon's strong arms around her were absorbing her shock.

"Just what was so upsetting about the wedding photo?" He grasped instinctively; there was something beyond the simple sight of the photograph.

Carol tried to steady herself, her regard for her mother in total ruins.

"Talk to me. Please," Damon begged.

She lifted her head and intercepted his brilliant down-bent gaze.

Sexual attraction asserted its sovereignty. Of a sudden, their proximity was stunning. A terrible longing flooded through her. She knew she shuddered, but such excitement was flashing through her, it was rocking her entire body. Their immediate world grew dim. It was so quiet, she could listen in to her own heart beat.

"Talk?" she heard herself murmur like a release. A little rivulet of heat-induced perspiration ran down between her breasts. The light perfume she was wearing rose like a fine mist around them.

It was too much, even for Damon. The lawyer in him knew he was risking much. He even had the feeling this could not possibly be happening. Not *now.* But he was pitched head-long into an intense sexual hunger that had been simmering from the moment he had laid eyes on her. From her expression, she was all but handing herself to him. It was an incitement too powerful to override.

He gathered her up more strongly into his arms. Her face was upturned to him. Her eyes had closed, but her lovely mouth was parted, open to his. He could *not* find the strength to resist.

She's your responsibility.

Again the voice of command. Only she was allowing this, caught in the grip of the same overwhelming excitement. The two of them might have been inhabitants of an alternate world. He closed his own eyes as he lowered his mouth onto hers, his lips closing around hers, the suppleness of them in-toxicating him. Her cheeks radiated heat. They were damp with tears. He tasted salt on his tongue. She didn't deny him. This was what they so burningly wanted.

He was taking the weight of her, revelling in the softness and delicacy of her body, alive and so responsive under his hands. One of his hands came up to cradle her nape. Her skin was as smooth as satin….

It was an agony and a ravishing pleasure. Both feelings co-existed. Both of them were wordless under the assault of the senses. He knew he should pull back, but all restraints were off. His desire for her had out-powered reason. They were kissing open-mouthed. Their tongues met in that inner space, a love dance as old as time. His free hand had slipped down of its own volition to cup one small perfect breast. He could feel the hardness of the nipple against his palm. The act of caressing her breast raised his level of desire.

All was heat, fragrance, the driving need to come together on a deeper more dangerous level. Soft little moans that issued from her mouth acted on him like a mating call. He was aware of his powerful erection, a man's compelling need to enter the body of the woman he desired. His blood was pumping madly. At that moment all he wanted in life was to take this beautiful young woman and make her his. Not for a day or a night but forever.

So strong were his feelings, no outside influence could make itself heard. Her body was so slight against the male strength and sheer weight of his. He couldn't get enough of her. His fingers slipped under the waist band of her cropped navy trousers.

I'd stop now, if I were you.

This time the voice inside his head compelled attention. *Stop.*

His eyes flew open. God knew, in kissing her he was complicating not only her existence but his. These weren't kisses born of compassion. They were kisses born of sexual hunger that had its own irresistible line of attack.

He had to tear his mouth from hers, but he still kept her held to his heart. It seemed to him his whole life had been moving towards this point.

Carol too was suspended in sensation. She lifted her head. "Did you just kiss me?" She was so aquiver with sensation, it was almost a torture.

"I surely did."

"Do you think it might happen again?" she whispered.

He tilted her chin. "At least it drove the tears away." He was astonished his voice sounded normal, when what he felt was an incredible exhilaration. "I hope I didn't startle you?"

"Only to the point where everything counted for nothing." She didn't care if the admission betrayed her. She was too far gone. "I've never in my life been kissed like that."

He kept his eyes on her lovely face. Her expression appeared overwrought. He wanted to kiss her again. He hadn't found the extra strength to free her, but he knew he had to call a stop. "Would you want to change anything?" He brushed back a few springy tendrils from her temples.

Carol took time to find an answer. "You could break my heart, Damon. I'd forgive you."

Her answer rocked him. For the second time he had to pitch a fierce battle for control. Eventually his sense of what was best for them won out. He lifted her to her feet. "I would never do that."

"Not deliberately. *No.*" Carol placed her hands against his chest.

"Not for anything. I know something about the wedding photo of your parents shocked you. Or it shocked a memory out of you. You promised me you'd tell me about everything that disturbs you. I'm going to hold you to that."

She knew he would. "I have to get things together in my own mind, Damon," she said in as calm a voice as she could muster.

"Okay, that's a start. I'm ready to listen whenever you want."

Words she desperately needed to get out choked in her throat. She needed time. "I suppose we'd better go back downstairs. They'll be wondering where we are."

"You don't have to account to anyone for your time, Carol. If you think you can manage the sack of baubles, I can manage the tree."

She picked up the large cotton sack filled with Christmas baubles, considering its weight. For all the contents, it was feather-light. "No problem. I'll lead the way." She smiled at him. A lovely smile, yet it trembled.

They had left their close and comfortable relationship way behind. That relationship had taken a giant leap into the unknown. Those ecstatic moments between them could not be taken back. Unforgettable as they were, it didn't guarantee ownership of one by the other or increasing intimacy between them. There were hazards ahead for both of them to overcome.

Amy Hoskins, the housekeeper, didn't know what to do. As far as she knew, all the house guests had arrived. She hurried into the drawing room where the whole party was enjoying drinks.

She addressed Maurice as a matter of course. "There's a Mr and Mrs Emmett at the gate, sir."

"Good Lord!" Maurice Chancellor's handsome face flushed. He turned his head. "Did you know about this, Carol?"

Was she supposed to apologize? Damon wondered, feeling hot under the collar. Maurice Chancellor was having a hard time remembering who actually owned Beaumont.

Carol hid her perturbation. What a Christmas this was going to be! "My mother never ceases to surprise me," she said, looking past her uncle to the housekeeper. "Go let them in, Mrs Hoskins."

Amy Hoskins didn't argue. She didn't know what might be in store for her if she got on the wrong side of 'the *heiress.*' That was what Mrs Chancellor always called her niece by marriage. No love lost there.

"I call that cheek!" Dallas cried out in a voice so cataclysmic it cut off all conversation. She hated, positively *hated* Roxanne—the woman who had everything she didn't. She would never forgive her husband for saying that. "So what will we do now?"

"Enjoy yourself as best you can, Dallas," Carol advised, wondering what her mother had done to earn so much hatred. "My mother is devoted to me."

Dallas was on the point of responding, only at the last minute she caught her husband's eye. It gave her fair warning. People always did mistake Maurice's superficial charm for weakness. They had no idea of his full weight. Any warmth Maurice projected was fake.

CHAPTER SIX

ROXANNE, LOOKING SIMPLY stunning, swept into the entrance hall, her manner that of a world-famous diva making an appearance.

"It's called making an entrance," Damon murmured in Carol's ear.

"And it's taken an awful lot of practice."

Roxanne acknowledged them with Euro-style kisses—longer, more lingering, on Damon's tanned cheek. "Lovely to see you again."

"May I wish you a Happy Christmas," Damon responded suavely.

Roxanne took that as a positive sign. "Looking forward to catching up later."

Without excuse or explanation, as was her wont, she bypassed those congregated in the drawing room with no more than a flourishing wave. Most of the guests were sitting agog, nursing a drink, as though it was intermission time at a theatre. Roxanne allowed her daughter to escort her and Jeff to the best of the remaining guest rooms.

"This won't do, Carol," Roxanne pronounced sharply, poised on the threshold as though refusing to go in. "Who's in the Yellow Suite?"

"Chazza and his wife," Carol mocked. "He's the short bald guy."

Roxanne frowned while Jeff supplied a name. "You know, Roxy—Chazza Millar."

"That old bore!" Roxanne exclaimed. "You'll have to find something better than this, Carol. I won't stay here."

"That's okay, Mother. You weren't *invited*."

"Never mind that." Roxanne brushed the lack of invitation off. "I'm your mother."

"When you *remember*. It does have an en suite. I can't shift anyone at this stage." Carol turned her head. "Would you stop leering at me, Jeff?"

"Not leering, love, *admiring*. You get more beautiful every day."

Roxanne rounded on him. "You really do amaze me, Jeff."

"Ditto," he said, unfazed.

"Well, I'll leave you to settle in," Carol said briskly, though she was barely coping with a whole raft of emotions. "Dinner at eight. It won't be held."

"Ah, for God's sake!" Roxanne cried in disgust. "No need to sound like your damned grandfather. It almost beggars belief how much you're getting like him."

"What about my *father,* Mother?" Carol hit back. "Can you remember him or have you completely wiped him out of your memory?"

"Steady on, Carol," Jeff intervened, seeing the hot flush that rose to his wife's cheeks. Many the object Roxy had hurled at him.

"Keep out of this, Jeff," Carol warned. For a moment there Carol had felt ready to lash out at her mother.

"All right, love." Jeff backed off. Little Carol had not just grown inches, she'd grown feet. "I told Roxy we wouldn't be welcome."

Carol stared at her mother with anger and bafflement in her eyes. "Why would you want to come? I'd have thought you'd be too wary of the ghosts."

Roxanne reacted with astonishment. "Ghosts? What ghosts?"

"The ghosts in the attic," Carol said.

Abruptly, as if her legs couldn't support her, Roxanne collapsed on the day bed. "What on earth are you talking about?"

"What's the matter, Mum? Have you remembered something?"

Roxanne shrugged her elegant shoulders. "What's to know?"

"Don't call me on that one," Carol said harshly. "We can discuss it another time. It will be perfectly okay if after that you want to leave." She started to walk away.

"Is there a point to all this, Carol?" Roxanne called after her. Her normally smooth, arrogant voice emerged jerkily.

"Oh, my God, yes," Carol said. "Settle in, Mother. It won't be a long stay."

The tree, at least, proclaimed Christmas. They erected it in the entrance hall where it was shown off in all its glittering glory with brilliant lights and laden with dazzling ornaments, the traditional mix of red, gold and green. Troy had even lent a hand, although he stood back while Damon and the obliging Chazza Millar set the tree in a huge emerald-green ceramic pot. Carol added the presents she had brought with her, beautifully boxed and packaged, to those already in place. It should have been a joyous occasion. Instead Carol felt that, if not for Damon, her life would be unravelling into chaos.

She could only feel a kind of horror at her memories. Such horror, it was difficult indeed to keep her composure. Only she knew she had to maintain some sort of a front.

Dinner went off reasonably well. The food and wine were excellent. Dallas didn't deign to speak a word to Roxanne but the hatred in the air was palpable. Roxanne had in fact caused a stir, coming down to dinner in a red evening dress with a deep V-neck that exposed a good deal of her creamy breasts. She looked as sexy as it was possible for a woman to look. Maurice couldn't take his eyes off her, along with every other man at the table—with the exception of Damon and Troy, who appeared impervious to Roxanne's undoubted charms.

"God, your mother's *gorgeous!*" Amanda told her later.

"She is indeed," Carol said, a knife in her heart.

The household didn't retire until well after midnight. Roxanne's presence, not entirely unexpected by Carol, undoubtedly added spice to the occasion. Roxanne for her part was clearly gaining wicked pleasure from totally eclipsing her former sister-in-law. In fact, Dallas was the first one to withdraw for the night.

"You know just what you are, don't you?" she hissed at Roxanne as she passed.

"Of course I do. And so do you, you frumpy old thing!" Roxanne shot back with a kind of benevolence. It was Christmas, after all. One had to rise to the occasion. One of the wives who had overheard the sotto-voce exchanges stood rooted to the spot, her face a study.

When the house was quiet, Carol went back downstairs. Far too many lights had been left on in her opinion. Their guests should be able to see if they came downstairs for any reason—and she couldn't think what—but she felt a clear responsibility to conserve energy. In the library, she twisted behind her, feeling a presence. Her cousin Troy was standing there. He was still dressed, without his tie, a few buttons on his shirt undone. He was smiling happily, a drunken smile.

"What is it, Troy?" She narrowed her eyes. "Is there something you want?" She couldn't help thinking Troy could well turn into a stalker. She was coming to realise her own cousin really fancied her.

"Why did you get that hair of yours cut?" he asked, his eyes ranging all over her. Like him, she was still dressed.

She looked utterly delectable, fantastic, sexy, stunning. The crystal decoration on her short gilded dress glittered like tiny diamonds in the light.

"You don't like it?" As though she cared.

He gave her an odd smile. He'd had a lot to drink at dinner, and afterwards with "the boys." "Don't get me wrong, you look terrific, but I did prefer that flaming mane."

"Well, this is easier," Carol said shortly. "So, I repeat, is there anything you want?" She leaned over to switch off a table lamp, unaware in the lamplight her hair had been shooting off ruby, gold and amber lights. "I have to say you've all got far too used to leaving on lights. At night, from a distance Beaumont must look like an ocean-going liner."

"So what's your problem?" he challenged, his manner aggressive. "The bills are paid on time."

"It's not that, Troy, it's conservation."

"Save the planet. Save the whales. Save the cows," he chortled. "And you're utterly determined on it, like poor old Grandfather."

"I am. Now, if you don't want anything, I'm going up to bed." Her eyes measured the distance to the door. She had the dismal feeling Troy could come after her with a mind to grab her.

She was so right. "Of course, Hunter will be joining you?" Troy laughed bitterly, not bothering to guard his jealousy.

"He will *not*. Not that it's any of your business."

"It *is* my business. We're family." His gaze locked on her brimming with unwelcome sexual attraction.

"That's a hoot."

Everything's okay, Carol. Just keep walking. This is your home. He's not going to attack you. He's just mad enough and drunk enough to want to kiss you. Maybe maul you.

She was on alert. Even then his move on her happened too fast.

"Let go of me," she ordered through gritted teeth. She was genuinely shocked.

"It's okay. I don't want to frighten you." He was surprisingly strong, wrestling her into his arms.

"You're not frightening me, you moron." His fingers were digging into her.

"God you've turned into a real little sexpot, haven't you?" Troy was breathing hard. "Don't worry, everything's going to be fine. A few kisses. A few hugs."

"Not in one-million light years."

Stop and think. What were you taught?

Her heart was pounding, but Carol let her body relax. She wanted to get him off-guard. Let him think she was giving up the struggle, or even playing some silly sex game. He must have thought so, because he gave a sickening laugh of triumph. It was her moment. Carol twisted sharply. She lifted her slender leg, kneeing him crunchingly hard in the groin.

He doubled over, his face contorted with pain. "You— You crazy bitch!"

"Shut up or I'll hit you with something hard." Carol gave him a good shove that sent him sprawling to the floor. "What a fool you are, Troy. Do you really think you can get away with molesting me?"

Troy was poleaxed by her action. Who would have thought it of little Carol? It was enough to make him freak out. "I just wanted…. I just wanted…to talk," he moaned, rolling over onto his side, his legs drawn up in agony.

Carol stood over him, her voice cold. "I want you out of here, Troy. Your girlfriend can stay. You make some excuse to leave in the morning."

She went to move away from him, thinking that was that, only he surprised her by making a grab for her leg. She almost tripped, thinking she might land in a heap, only he wound his hand tightly around her ankle. "Gotcha!" There was no

time to take a breath. With his tight grasp on her ankle, she
couldn't risk trying to use her other leg to kick out at him.
She only had her hands. She wanted to pound him and pound
him. How dared he? How dared any man attack a woman?
She wasn't in the least frightened. She was prepared to defend herself.

"What the hell is going on here?" Damon's voice boomed
across the dimly lit room.

Carol didn't answer. She bent down, taking a flat-handed
swipe at Troy's head. "Let go of my ankle."

He did so immediately, at the same time throwing her off
backwards. She slammed into Damon. "Get up, Chancellor,"
Damon rasped, steadying her.

Troy's response was a whine. "Do you believe it? She
bloody well attacked me."

Damon put Carol aside, then moved to jerk Troy to his
feet. "What were you planning?" he asked, his voice a deep
growl in his throat. He was just barely containing his outrage.

"Don't talk to *me* like that," Troy shouted. "Who the hell
are you, Hunter? *I'm* a Chancellor. For your information, I
wasn't planning anything. I came down just like Carol to turn
off a few lights—conservation, dear boy."

Damon seized him by his shirt front, almost lifting Troy
off his feet. "Don't 'dear boy' me, you sick piece of work.
This was a premeditated move on your own cousin. You saw
Carol coming downstairs, so you followed her. The miracle
is I had the sure feeling you'd try something, especially when
you got yourself drunk over dinner. I heard your father speaking pretty sternly to you. I checked out my hunch—I rely on
them. Don't look so surprised, Chancellor. You're not very
good at hiding your attraction to Carol. It's apparent to a lot
of people, not just me."

"What about you, big boy?" Troy tried to wrench himself
away, bellowing into Damon's face. "Nothing's going to stop

you. You want her for yourself. You might fool some people—they think you're this great guy, so bloody brilliant—but you don't fool me. Who trusts a lawyer anyway? You know what Shakespeare said—*the first thing we do, let's kill all the lawyers.* If you landed Carol, which is your aim, you'd never have to do a day's work again."

"Not doing a day's work again is a dismaying prospect," Damon said, controlling his temper. "Unlike you, I enjoy my work. My role is to look out for all of Carol's interests. I don't have your *inglorious* ambitions."

Troy swore violently.

"Watch your language, pal," Damon warned him.

"I've figured you out, Hunter." Troy glared back. "I don't like you. I never did."

"I'm seriously worried." Damon turned to Carol. "What do you want done about this guy? I don't think he should stay."

"Troy will be leaving in the morning, won't you, Troy?" Carol said. "I propose you get an early start."

"I'm not sure it's your wisest decision to make an enemy of me, Carol," Troy said heavily, still in physical pain.

Damon intervened before Carol could answer. "If that's a threat, I know what to do about it."

"Ah, the big-time lawyer again!" Troy sneered. "Always at the ready to defend his favourite client. I'm on to you, Hunter. So are a lot of other people. Shocking, how you let Amber Coleman down when you let her believe you were going to marry her. Only you found someone better—little Carol here, the heiress. I'll be pleased to leave in the morning. I'll leave Summer behind, if you don't mind. She's cute but she doesn't have much in the way of a brain."

"Neither do you, Troy," Carol said. "And you're definitely not cute. It's your actions that brought this on you. They were way out of line. I have no romantic interest in you, nor could

I ever have. I'm amazed you thought otherwise. Quite apart from anything else, you're my first cousin."

That didn't appear to bother Troy. In fact, he seemed to find it amusing. "Not a problem these days, sweetheart. That knee-kick of yours was first rate to bring a man down. Where did you learn it?"

"From a master," Carol said briefly. "And that's not all in my bag of tricks. Happy Christmas, Troy. I don't think anyone is going to miss you terribly. Maybe your mother."

"At least she's not a notorious con woman like Roxanne," Troy retorted with venom.

"Keep your remarks to yourself," Carol said coldly.

"She ruins men, that woman," Troy shouted. "My mother has told me all about her. She really hates her."

Carol didn't respond. She was well aware of Dallas's hatred.

They stood silently until Troy's footsteps had died away. "I'm glad you wanted to make sure I was okay." Carol turned to Damon. *Had he promised marriage to Amber Coleman?*

It seemed to Damon her expression was very searching.

"I'm finding it hard to believe what just happened," she said.

"It doesn't need much explaining, Carol. Your cousin finds you extremely attractive. He doesn't see your relationship as a barrier. I think he was seeing keeping all the money in the family."

"Dear God!" Carol sighed. "How did he ever get to be so arrogant? Everything he wants, he gets. Did you hear what he said about my mother, the notorious con woman?"

Damon could hear the pain and the shame in her voice. "I can only assume that has a lot to do with his mother's jealousy of Roxanne. It borders on paranoia."

"I suppose it does. Dallas is going to be furious Troy is being sent home."

"If she feels so strongly, maybe she can go with him," Damon suggested. "Your uncle can look after his guests. He doesn't appear all that close to either his wife or his son." He steered Carol into an armchair, turning a table lamp back on.

Carol felt enormously distressed. She was shaking but she wasn't crying. She had defended herself very well. "All those sessions at the gym paid off."

"I'm only sorry I didn't have the pleasure of witnessing the way you brought him down."

She stared up at him. "Nevertheless, he would have eventually overpowered me. I'm so glad you turned up when you did."

"Is that the only reason you sound so unhappy?"

She shrugged. "Life's a struggle, isn't it, Damon? Having a lot of money doesn't help. People don't think you deserve it. They want to take it off you. Are you after my money, Damon?"

His expression grew taut. "To be honest, Carol, I wish you didn't have it."

"Really?" She thought he meant it. But did she really know Damon as well as she thought? Did anyone even know the person closest to them? From her own experience the answer was no. Her head was saying one thing, her heart another. But hearts weren't to be trusted. Too many hearts had seen their dreams dissolve.

"Yes, really. We're attracted to one another. I can't possibly be *that* wrong?"

"And I can't possibly deny it."

"Do you want to deny it? You have only to tell me, Carol. You're young. You have so many issues to cope with, so much to learn. I don't fancy putting any pressure on you. What happened, happened. I didn't have the power to stop it. But I can and will in future. I was caught off-guard."

He looked very much on his mettle. "Don't get angry, Damon. I know that."

"I hope so." His sombre expression didn't change. "Our attraction obviously shows. Plenty of people would be trying to figure out my 'agenda,' as Troy called it. You're right about Amber Coleman—she's a born troublemaker. She'll do as much damage as she can. Your cousin will help her—they must keep in touch. Obviously, Troy has put doubts about me into your mind. I can only tell you Amber Coleman and I never came remotely close to discussing marriage. For that matter, I've never talked marriage with any woman." He was shattered to think she mightn't believe him. But there was nothing he could do about it if she didn't.

"That's not why I'm sad, Damon."

"Then tell me. I'm being completely honest with you, Carol. I'd like you to be honest with me. What's really causing your upset? I have a strong feeling it's what you've remembered about that day in the attic when you were a little girl."

She stared into his eyes. They were so dark, yet lustrous, as if a light were behind them. "If I tell you, you must promise me you'll tell no one else."

Instantly Damon the lawyer was wary. "I don't know if I *can* promise that, Carol. Did someone harm you, God forbid?"

She covered her eyes with her hands, much like a child. "I did go up to the attic on my own," she confided. "I wanted to explore. It's such a marvellous place, even now. I was a very imaginative child. I did think someone might come after me—my nanny—but it wasn't nanny and they weren't after *me*. They wanted to be alone. As soon as I saw them, I hid behind a chest. I was just a child but I knew what was happening." She uncovered her eyes looking up at him. Her blue eyes grew wide as she told Damon what she had seen. It was so very, very *wrong*.

*   *   *

Breakfast was served between seven and nine. Carol stayed away the whole time. She had orange juice, tea and toast in her room. She wasn't in the least hungry; she hadn't had a good night. Why would she have? At long last she had discovered the truth. Was her beloved father a victim of the truth? She would die herself finding out.

Her mother and Jeff were in their room.

"What do *you* want?" Roxanne asked in surprise. She was wearing a lacy white top with white skinny jeans, her glossy dark hair drawn back from her face. She really was a beautiful woman, on the *outside*.

"A talk with you, Roxanne," Carol said, while looking at Jeff. "Do you mind, Jeff? This is private. I should warn you, afterwards I want you both to leave. You've had breakfast. You're *not* staying for Christmas dinner."

Roxanne broke into a derisive laugh.

"What's the problem, love?" Jeff looked at his stepdaughter, his expression earnest. He really was very fond of Carol. He was only human. He couldn't help it if he thought her a luscious little thing. But he would *never* hurt her.

"That's between my mother and me, Jeff. If you wouldn't mind leaving."

Jeff shook his head. "If you want me to, I will," he said. "You're going to be okay?"

"Of course she is, Jeff, don't be so stupid." Roxanne turned on him scathingly.

"Come off it, Roxy. We all know you're a total bitch."

Roxanne laughed bitterly. "Divorce me, then."

"Maybe I will." Jeff walked to the door, shutting it hard after him.

Roxanne now turned on Carol, her anger powerful to see. "So what is it? Don't you just love being in a position to throw your weight around?" she accused.

"There are times when I'm glad of it, Roxanne."

"Not *Mother?*"

"You haven't been much of a mother to me," Carol said without emotion. "You weren't much of a wife to my father, either. Even Jeff could leave you."

"Do you really think I'd care?" Roxanne scoffed. "Plenty more where he came from. What is it you want to talk to me about?"

"I think you know already," Carol said. "That day in the attic when I caught you and Uncle Maurice kissing passionately. *You*—my mother, my father's wife—*he*, my uncle. My father was away with Poppy on a business trip."

Roxanne's flawless skin took on a deep flush. But she'd had time to come up with her explanation. "So you saw us?" she said as though it was of little consequence. "Nothing much happened. I can't help it when men fall in love with me. They do it all the time."

"Uncle Maurice *hurt* me," Carol said, feeling the imprint of his fingers on her delicate five-year-old shoulders.

"He did not!" Roxanne rejected that out of hand. "He only dragged you out from behind that chest. He might have given you a few shakes."

"He said if I told anyone bad things would happen to me," Carol reminded her mother. "He shook me very hard. He made me cry. You didn't stop him. My own mother didn't stop him."

"I was going to." Roxanne tried to defend herself. "But Carol, I was in shock. If you had talked to anyone, Adam or your grandfather, think of the damage you could have done."

"When the damage you did was just dreadful. I don't know how you can live with it. Were you in love with Uncle Maurice?" She had to realise her uncle was even now a very handsome man.

Roxanne responded with great bitterness. "At least he was more in love with me than your father."

"So that's why Dallas hates you. She knew."

"She didn't know," Roxanne shot back sullenly. "She guessed. We women are good at guessing, but she never, ever had proof. We were extremely careful. You were the only one to surprise us. In a way, it was your own fault. You always were a little monkey." An odd expression flitted across her face. "Do you realise Maurice could very well be your *father?*"

Carol was so shocked she felt a pain in her chest and a tightness in her throat. "That is the most wicked lie!" she gasped.

"Is it?" Roxanne countered, collapsing on the chintz upholstered bench at the end of the bed. "*Think,* Carol. You mightn't be the Chancellor heiress after all."

"For God's sake, don't you know? Were you having sex with both brothers?"

Roxanne laced her long fingers together. "The short answer is, yes. I've always been a highly sexed woman. Adam was always away with your grandfather, the favoured son, the one most like him. That's the way it goes, isn't it? Parents favour the child most like them."

"Obviously. You never favoured *me.* There's such a thing as DNA, you know."

"Can they really tell the difference in the DNA of brothers?" When Roxanne looked up, she actually had tears in her eyes.

"Crocodile tears, Mother." Roxanne was a born actor, like all narcissists. "I'm reasonably certain they can. Now you're in your confessing mode, tell me, did you and Uncle Maurice plan on pushing my father overboard?"

Roxanne could barely collect herself. "Don't remind me of the *worst* day of my life, Carol. Adam was the love of my

life. It was a terrible accident. I was such a ninny on boats.
Adam never did show me what to do in case of an accident. I
never thought there could be one. He was a very experienced
yachtsman. I went into a complete panic—it paralysed me.
I ran down to the back of the boat to unfasten the lifebuoy
but it remained attached. I started pitching everything that
would float into the water for him to grab hold of. But the
boat kept on going. Adam was in the water. I couldn't swim.
God! It was a ghastly experience. I wouldn't wish it on my
worst enemy. And there was more to come."

"A lot of people didn't believe you," Carol supplied bleakly.
She had to wait for her mother to collect herself. Roxanne
appeared distraught for the first time Carol was witness to.

"There was a good reason for that. I was too beautiful and
too rich. There are big downsides to both. Another thing, I
keep my emotions hidden. I didn't play the weeping widow.
People demand that. I did the opposite. I had done no wrong,
but I didn't look *right*. I was condemned for that. Your grandfather acted like the hanging judge. Your so-sensitive little
grandmother accused me to my face. I told her, I *swore,* I
wasn't capable of such a thing. I wasn't capable of *murder.*"

"They say we all are, given enough provocation," Carol
said with grim horror. "Wives shoot their long-abusive hus-
bands."

"I'm all for that." Roxanne pulled herself together. In her
own way she was a strong woman. But in the space of minutes she looked older, more vulnerable. "I'm innocent, Carol.
Believe that if nothing else. As for who your biological father
is, I genuinely *don't* know."

"God!" Carol felt her sense of shock mounting to a mind-
bending level. "But I look like my father." She felt so sick,
she thought she might pass out.

"Listen to you, Carol!" Roxanne cried out as though Carol
were completely stupid. "Adam and Maurice both had deep-

blue eyes and that red-setter hair. You look like *both* of them. You must know that. Unfortunately, you got your grandmother's height. She was a fey little thing, wasn't she? No one was surprised when she took her own life."

Carol rallied. "Leave my grandmother out of this, Roxanne," she said, beyond being shocked by her mother. "At least we know she *is* my grandmother. She was a lovely lady, too sensitive for the likes of you and Dallas. Think how much help two supportive daughters-in-law might have been. Instead of that, she got you two."

"So what do we do now?" Roxanne conjectured. "As far as I'm concerned, we share this secret. You wouldn't want to lose your grand inheritance. I wouldn't want you to lose it. You *are* my daughter. It would all go to Maurice, that gutless wimp. He was going to divorce Dallas, you know."

"After which you would marry him?" Carol couldn't jettison her suspicions, for all her mother's tearful explanations. Perhaps her father's death had not been premeditated. It couldn't have been engineered by Roxanne, but when face to face with a life-changing opportunity could she have allowed her husband's body to slip away? Where was the evidence to say she hadn't?

Shame on you, Carol.

"Maurice was a better lover than Adam. As for Jeff, whatever mojo he had, he's lost. The two of them have one thing in common—lots of money."

Carol took successive deep breaths. "Do you know, Roxanne, I think you're really *sick*. We're going to share our secret, are we? I think not. You would have something to hold over me. It wouldn't take you long before you started into blackmail. Now, I'll leave you to pack your things." Carol started walking to the door. "I want you and Jeff out of here within the hour. I'll sort my own life out, I promise you. We'll be in touch."

* * *

When she went downstairs some time later, she found Amanda and Summer standing in front of the Christmas tree in the entrance hall. Their heads were together. They were in deep conversation like long-time friends. Such were the curiosities of life. Both looked up in relief as they saw Carol descend the staircase.

Honouring her allotted role in life, Amanda was the first to speak. "Caro, what's going on here?" she asked, her expressive face agog. "Troy took off, leaving Summer in the lurch—"

"Not that I mind in the least," Summer broke in. "You did say I could stay, Carol?" she asked, looking embarrassed.

"You're very welcome, Summer," Carol said warmly, joining them in front of the glittering tree surrounded by yet-unopened presents. What a Christmas!

"What about your mother and stepfather?" Amanda asked. "Give it to us straight-up. They whizzed past ten minutes ago. We were standing here. Your mother ignored us like we were the lowest of the low. She sure didn't shout Christmas. But Jeff wished us a merry Christmas. He didn't look too merry, either. Have they left?" Amada sounded like she was delighted to see them go.

"They have, Amanda. Pressing business for Jeff."

"Over Christmas?" Amanda's tone went up a couple of notches. "You're kidding me."

"Well, they've gone. That's the bottom line." She looked them over. "Where are you two going?" Both girls wore casual T-shirts and jeans, trainers on their feet.

"We thought we'd explore," Amanda said, giving her new best friend a smile. "You have a whole big botanical park out there, and woodlands. Then we plan a bit of a run around. That's if I can borrow your car. This place is so *beautiful,* Carol. No wonder Troy talks about it all the time."

"Does he? And there I was thinking he's strictly an indoors man. Take the car, by all means. It's not locked. The key is under the mat of the driver's seat. There's plenty of petrol. You'll be back in time for Christmas dinner, of course?"

"You bet!" Both girls said together. This was the ritziest place both could ever imagine.

"By the way, Damon was looking for you," Amanda said. "You two look great together."

"Don't be silly, Amanda. There is absolutely nothing going on between Damon and me. He's my lawyer and a very good friend."

Amanda gave her a huge grin. "I reckon he aims to be a whole lot more than that. Friendship doesn't always continue in a straight line, kiddo. Damon is every girl's dream."

CHAPTER SEVEN

CAROL WALKED TO the rear of the house to the informal living area, a light-filled family area with a series of tall French doors on two walls affording views over the beautiful rear gardens. Maurice, a stony-faced Dallas and their smiling friends were seated comfortably in very comfortable custom-made sofas and armchairs upholstered in cream with a robust blue stripe.

The men jumped to their feet as soon as she walked in. Everyone was appropriately attired for a festive Christmas. She greeted them all pleasantly—even Dallas—wished them a Happy Christmas, made small talk— she was getting very good at it—and told them presents would be opened before Christmas dinner which would start at 2:00 p.m.

"I'm off for a walk now," she said, giving a parting wave. "See you then."

"A moment, Carol." Maurice closed the short distance between them, taking her arm in avuncular fashion. "A few words, if I may?"

"Of course, Uncle Maurice."

They moved off. The others went back to their conversation. There was lots to talk about. Everyone considered that Maurice Chancellor was behaving in an exemplary manner, considering he had been bypassed by his own father for his young niece. Not that she didn't look or sound capable of picking up the reins. They had all been surprised by Carol's considerable intelligence, her grasp on both legal and business matters. She had considerable presence for one so young. A Chancellor, of course, bred in the bone.

Maurice directed Carol to his study, or what had been his father's study. He continued to use it as his own. His niece—highly intelligent, admittedly—was but a slip of a girl. Would to God he'd had a daughter like that! Troy was such a disappointment, ruined by his mother.

"Take a seat, Carol," he invited.

She moved into a leather armchair facing the massive desk. Maurice retreated behind it, putting several feet between them. The cedar-panelled room was very impressive. There was a *hush* to it, like an exclusive men's club.

"You first, Uncle Maurice," she said, not about to waste a moment on politeness. That was all over. She felt exhausted beyond merely physical. She was mentally exhausted. What more was there for her to learn? Whatever it was, she couldn't shrink from it.

"Whatever do you mean, 'you first'?" he asked in astonishment.

"Exactly what I said. I assume you have a problem with my mother's leaving?"

He actually laughed. "I had a problem with your mother *coming,* my dear girl. Roxanne and I had little to say to each other for years."

"Far cry from the old days?" she said bluntly.

He appeared staggered. "Carol, I don't know what you mean."

"You hoped I'd never remember, didn't you?" Carol said. "You thought you'd frightened me into forgetting. You shook me and shook me, a five-year-old girl. You *threatened* me, come to that."

"Carol." He stretched out an imploring hand.

"Don't deny it," she said sharply, jerking back. "The truth is finally out. You and my mother were having an affair. I caught you kissing and fondling one another. Even as a child I knew that was all wrong."

Maurice Chancellor bent his tawny head, as though in shame. "Carol, I am *so* sorry."

"Who would believe you?" she said bleakly. "All you and my mother were sorry about was being caught. No wonder Dallas hates her."

Maurice lifted his head. "Dallas didn't know." He sounded emphatic.

"Maybe she didn't know, but she guessed. The same old story—a woman's intuition. I don't even know if the grand affair came to an end after my father's death."

"Of course it did. Adam's death was a tragedy for us all, not just my parents. I was always very envious of Adam— my father and my mother loved him far better than me—but I knew it wasn't his fault. I loved my brother. I want you to believe that."

"But you had no difficulty deceiving him with his own wife?"

"God help me, I did," Maurice groaned. "It was quite unforgivable, I know. But Roxanne was such a temptress, the ultimate provocateur. She does it on purpose, always flaunting her powers. She knew I got nothing much in the way of sex from Dallas—little love from my parents, even from my own son. He's nothing more than a spoiled rotten dilettante. Roxanne was a *huge* mistake."

"She said you intended to divorce Dallas." Carol trained her eyes on him.

"That'll be the day!" The glance he returned spoke volumes. "I was never going to divorce Dallas. My dear wife knew that well enough. So did Roxanne. Roxanne wasn't even confident of my brother. Beautiful as she is, Adam was fast falling out of love with her. I understand that now. The sad thing is, Roxanne is indifferent to all feelings other than her own. Surely you've noticed? Adam was madly in love with Roxanne when they married. I was totally bewitched myself. In her way, she's an extraordinary woman."

"But the spell wears off?" Carol had seen that for herself.

"It certainly wore off with Adam and with me. That episode in my life is blessedly behind me. I shouldn't be in the least surprised if Roxanne and Jeff are about to call it a day. Jeff is not a happy man."

"Neither are *you*. Neither is Troy."

"Now, that's what I wanted to talk to you about," Maurice said, leaning forward.

"Then talk."

"Troy told me he fears Damon Hunter is getting too close to you personally. I have to say, he's a truly exceptional young man. I like him. He's extremely clever, ambitious and handsome enough to turn any young woman's head."

"Agreed. So Troy came to you with my best interests at heart?"

"Of course. We're family. You have to be on the alert for fortune hunters, Carol. Hunter by name, hunter by nature. It would be an enormous coup for him. For all his cleverness he doesn't come from money. *Real* money. His mother ran a catering business, for God's sake."

Carol swept his snobbish comments aside. "The jarring truth is Troy, your son, tried to come on to me." God forbid Troy should be her half brother, she thought with a shudder. "Damon intervened after I gave Troy a good knee in the groin."

Maurice fell back in his chair. "Well, bully for you! You're actually telling me Troy tried something on with you?"

"Like father, like son."

Maurice flushed a dull red. "I deserve that. I had no idea

Troy had such feelings. Damn it all, you're first cousins! Now, don't you worry about this. I'll put him straight and I won't waste time. Incest is just too much."

"It wouldn't be that."

"Close enough in my book." Maurice Chancellor made a sound of disgust. "That boy is going fast to nowhere. His mother has ruined him. I told her over and over." He pushed himself to his feet. "You've been very badly done by, Carol. But I feared contacting Roxanne to get to you, my niece. I was such a coward on a number of counts. I thought you might remember and start telling people. Some people don't listen to children. Some do. The thing is we *all* should. That's it, Carol—your uncle is a coward."

Carol braced herself. "Do you believe my mother had nothing to do with my father's death?"

"God, yes! Roxanne went utterly to pieces. It was no play-acting, I assure you."

"How can you say that when at the will reading you practically accused my mother of wrongdoing and Dallas, needless to say, backed you up?"

He looked briefly sheepish. "A bit of play-acting on my part. I don't care to get on the wrong side of my dear wife. She knows too much. The thing is, Carol, we all needed someone to blame. My mother especially. She adored Adam. He was the son most sympathetic to her and her oddities. And, let's face it, she was quite odd. Roxanne didn't let your father drown, Carol. Roxanne couldn't do such a thing."

Couldn't she?

"Break their hearts, yes," Maurice continued. "The big trouble was, no one liked Roxanne. Women were very jealous of her. She actually went out of her way to make them jealous. She paid the price."

"So did your brother. Face up to it," Carol said in a toneless voice. She hesitated a moment, then plunged in. "You couldn't possibly be *my* father, could you?"

"What do you say?" Maurice looked stupefied.

"Think for a moment. My mother was having sex with both of you."

Maurice Chancellor's unlined skin turned ruddier as his blood-pressure soared. "I draw the line here, Carol."

"You should have drawn it *then*."

"I could *now*. Not a chance *then*. I was still a young man, or young enough. Roxanne reeled me in hook, line and sinker. We *always* used protection."

"Doesn't always work," Carol said dismally.

Maurice walked back behind the desk and dropped down heavily into the swivel chair. "Roxanne suggested this, of course? I see her hand in it."

"Maybe she doesn't know herself."

"Oh, get real!" Maurice was lost in moody contemplation. "Roxanne always has an agenda. She would have blackmailed me. She wanted me to leave Dallas. I told her I *couldn't*. I didn't want her to leave Adam, for that matter. It was a mad and utterly despicable interlude. Tell me, when does Roxanne ever accept the word *couldn't?*"

He had a powerful point. "Would you agree to DNA testing?"

"God, Carol!" He shot her a despairing look.

"For your brother's sake. For my sake. For your sake. We must determine the truth. Or maybe you think *truth* is a joke word?"

Maurice shook his handsome tawny head. "You *are* your father's daughter, Carol. Roxanne lives to stir up trouble. She knows how to push everyone's buttons. She's jealous of you. You're young and beautiful—you've got so much more in the way of intellect than she ever had. That includes integrity. But, if it sets your mind at rest, I agree to DNA testing."

* * *

Afterwards she went in search of Damon. Who else did she have to turn to? She was aware Damon had pulled back, as if regretting the massive shift in their relationship. She hoped it was because of his scruples—the thought it might throw a fragile balance into disorder. He was her lawyer and the man her grandfather had appointed to look out for her and her interests. She could understand he would be troubled by the gossip that was already doing the rounds. Amber Coleman had it in for her. So would Troy, now that she had rejected his unwanted advances. Damon had moved a few paces back to combat it. She had to accept he knew what was best for them both, but his decision had left her feeling very forlorn.

Maybe falling in love really was a madness. She hadn't seen it coming. She had the strong feeling Damon hadn't see it coming, either. The attraction had taken them by storm. It had been instant and urgent. *Whoever loved that loved not at first sight?* There was overwhelming evidence of that. That didn't mean the going would be easy or even turn out well. She needed to speak to Damon. She needed his legal advice apart from the comfort of his presence.

She found him in the last place she looked, taking laps of the turquoise pool. As she expected, he was a strong swimmer, with a powerful, even stroke that had him gliding through the water. He didn't see her until he was pulling himself with ease out of the pool.

"Hi!" She thought she had never seen a better male body. He had such a physicality to him, such a fluid grace of movement, especially for a tall man. His broad, naked chest had a light matting of dark hair, ripples of hard muscle. There was an indent to his waist. His hips were taut. Her eyes ran over his lean, muscled arms, down the straight columns of his legs. As upset as she was, she still felt the erotic disturbances deep inside her. He was just so beautiful to her, one magnificent male creature.

"Hi, yourself!" His teeth were a white flash in his sun-bronzed face. He appeared to be gilded all over. The top band of his black swimming briefs had slipped down a few inches and there was no paler layer of skin. He grabbed a towel. He was quite unselfconscious, drying himself off before securing the towel around his waist. "That was great!" He swept his wetly gleaming dark hair back off his forehead. "Just what I needed. I have to confess, breakfast was so good I ate more than I normally do."

"And Christmas dinner to come. May I speak to you, Damon?"

"Need you ask?" He indicated two of the upholstered teak lounge chairs set around the perimeter of the pool and the adjoining pool house. Dry enough, he pulled on a white cotton shirt, leaving it unbuttoned. "You look stressed." She also looked a dream in her gauzy buttercup-yellow dress. To protect her porcelain skin, she wore a wide-brimmed straw hat, decorated with yellow-and-white silk hibiscus on her head. So feminine! That was the romantic look he loved above all.

"Wake-up time, Damon," she answered, showing a hint of her forlornness. "I know you'll be as shocked as I was, but my mother came out with an astonishing coda to what I've already told you." She paused, as though unable to go on.

"And?"

"Since I was a child, trauma has trailed me like a shadow—my father's tragic death, all the gossip about my mother. The trauma has reached a new height. My mother was not only having an affair with Uncle Maurice, she said—"

"Go on," he urged. "Obviously what she said deeply distressed you."

She lifted her blue eyes to him, the colour rivalling the burning blue of the sky. "Distress doesn't cover it. I was stunned out of my mind. She told me she didn't know for sure if Adam was my father. He could have been Maurice."

For a split second the ramifications of that exploded in Damon's head. Carol mightn't be the Chancellor heiress after all! If so, the will would be overturned. Maurice Chancellor would inherit. That would change *everything*. He could feel free to court her. As it was now, he was acutely aware of the big divide between them—wealth even more than her youth. He knew the guys she dated were fellow students, but Carol was very mature for her age. Within seconds, the bubble burst. His momentary elation was wiped out by her very real distress.

"Knowing your mother, Carol, she could simply be talking up trouble," he said comfortingly. "She likes to upset you. You have to speak to your uncle. I can come with you."

"Ah, Damon! I've already spoken to Uncle Maurice. He doesn't deny the affair. He says it's 'blessedly long over.' He's adamant Adam was my father. He's agreed to DNA testing."

"Well, that's significant, surely? God what a shock for you, Carol." Shock after shock. Damon's brow creased. "If Maurice *is* your father—and we're pretty sure he's *not*—it means he can contest your grandfather's will."

"I realise that, Damon." She showed not a great deal of concern. "I might *not* be the Chancellor heiress."

His dark gaze glittered over her. "Can you tell me how you feel about that?"

Carol didn't hesitate. "The most important thing is to establish who fathered me. I never have cared about all the money. Money is to be used to do good. When I'm an old lady, I want to be able to say I did my very best."

"And you will," he foretold. "I believe in you."

There was such sincerity in his voice. "So you believe I am who I'm supposed to be?"

His handsome mouth twisted. "Might be easier for me if you weren't."

Her heart took off like a bird in joyous flight. "What does that mean?"

He wanted to speak out, but he *knew* he had to keep himself on track. "First things first, Carol. Your mother is a born provocateur."

"Uncle Maurice said the same thing." Was it only a dream she had, she and Damon? Yet surely there had been something in his face, something deeply caressing that caught at her heart?

"He knows her well," Damon was saying. So had Selwyn Chancellor. The old man must have been absolutely sure Carol was Adam's daughter, the person to grow into the position of wisely administering the Chancellor fortune. Clearly he hadn't had the same faith in his younger son.

She felt unwilling to meet his eyes now, reined back by intuitive reserve. The last thing she wanted was to embarrass him. "I suppose we'd better go back. There are the presents to be distributed." She tried to recompose her face, only he suddenly reached out, caught the point of her chin and kissed her, as if the feel of her mouth against his gave him enormous pleasure. He might have been drinking in ambrosia fit for the gods. She closed her eyes so she, too, could record the moment of glowing rapture.

Steady now. Easy now, warned the voice in Damon's head, only he was being pulled under by the ever-widening ripples of excitement. Was there a name for this craving?

Of course there was.

It was *love.* Only, cravings were never satiated. They had to be constantly fed.

When he finally let her go, her whole body was quivering. "That was unexpected," Carol managed with a gasp.

"You have the power to bind, Carol." His answer was very serious.

The moment was almost painful to her. "I don't want to lose you, Damon. Not now. Not ever. You've become my rock."

He was so deeply moved he drew her to her feet, pulling the pretty straw hat off her head. "How beautiful you are!" So much beauty, so much delicacy in the porcelain perfection of her skin. He had to try very hard to dissipate the intensity of his desire.

She felt tears spring into her eyes. "You say that like it's a problem."

He looked away over her radiant head, the sun picking out gold and amber highlights. "In a sense it is—your beauty, your youth and your wealth."

"Do you wish it otherwise?" She caught his hand, staring up into his brilliant dark eyes. She was willing him to focus on her. Only his handsome features had drawn taut.

"These are the things I have to remember, Carol." His tone was slightly gritty.

"Maybe the way you kiss me gives the lie to your words." She was driven to challenge.

"Maybe it does." He was breathing deeply to steady his pulse.

Carol unclasped her hand, took her sunhat from him and settled it back on her head. It was essential not to embarrass him but she was sick to death of the supposedly moral hazards.

They began to walk back slowly to the house. Only Carol couldn't stop the excitement from pouring into her body like the golden sunbeams that were beating down on them. Try as she might, there didn't seem to be an escape from it. Her confidence soared one moment only to be shot down the next.

He took her hand. "Have I upset you?" He bent his head, trying to see beneath the wide brim of her hat.

"*Everything* about me is wrong," she said with a little laugh. "How very perverse." They were rounding the southern end of the garden. Innumerable buds of the Little Gem magnolias were bursting into flower, a waxy, creamy white against the glossy dark-green leaves with their purple undersides. Further on, arguably the most gorgeous of all tropical plants—the *Medinilla magnifica*—made a fantastic display with its hanging flower clusters, deep-pink flowers, mauve-pink bracts and purple-and-yellow stamens. She stopped to admire them. She wasn't ready yet to go into the house. Her pulses were still throbbing, at odds with her feigned composure.

"How easy it is to exalt in such beauty and profusion," Damon said.

His hand fell on her shoulder. It seemed like a very intimate gesture. She could feel the *heat* of it burning through to her skin. She heard him sigh. There was such a *silence* between them, yet it was crowded with unspoken words. She thought she could detect the strong beat of his heart.

"What are we doing, Damon?" She turned fully so she could stare up into his dark eyes.

He sighed again. "I can't tell you. The main thing, Carol, is keeping you safe."

"*Safe?*" She did something foolish then; she wasn't strong enough to resist. She turned her head so she could lay her cheek against his hand. Butterflies rose all around them in swarms, drunk on the flowers: the electric-blue Ulysses; the Golden Cruisers; the Lace Wings; the huge Bird Wings, Australia's largest species of butterfly, the female with a wing span of twenty centimetres. So big were they, they were slower in flight than the gorgeous Ulysses. The warm breeze shook out the myriad scents. It was so soporific, they might have fallen into a dream pocket where they were hidden from the world.

Discipline was proving far too exhausting for Damon. He drew her supple body fully into his arms, bending his gleaming dark head to kiss her so deeply it was as if he sought to imprint himself on her heart and her soul. There was no space between them, no indecision… This was a profoundly *private* moment, just for the two of them.

Carol had no idea how much time passed. It could have been moments, hours, a lifetime with one's deepest feelings unmasked. Desire had drawn them out and beyond themselves. But there was a greater desire—the desire for *more*.

The Christmas presents were distributed later on to the usual ooh's and aah's. Carol presented Damon with a very expensive rollerball pen. He had bought her a late-nineteenth-century Meissen model of Venus and Cupid, a lovely piece he'd had the good fortune to source.

"I love it, love it, love it!" She stood on tiptoes to kiss him on both cheeks. That apparently was acceptable to the rest. Such lightness of being! Only Damon could give her that.

It was nearing two o'clock and Amanda and Summer still hadn't returned.

"We'll have to start without them," Dallas said, sniffing her displeasure. "Have they no manners, no consideration? Why weren't *you* with them?" It sounded for all the world like she was deeply disappointed.

"If you must know, Dallas, it was an on-the-spot decision." Carol stared back. Dallas was positively pulsating with rage. It was becoming something of a defining characteristic. Obviously she was furious her adored son, Troy, had been sent on his way. Dallas had seen him off, no doubt heaping dire imprecations on Carol's head. Carol had the feeling Dallas hated her almost as much as she hated her mother, Roxanne.

Only, where *were* Amanda and Summer? They should have been back well before this.

"I'm going to tell the cook to serve the entrée," Dallas said like a woman who brooked no opposition.

"I suppose you should."

It was another half hour, when the guests were well into a lavish Christmas feast, when Mrs Hoskins came into the dining room, heading for Maurice, who sat in the seat of honour as host, with Carol at the other end.

Damon, to Carol's right, waited to see how she would handle this. "I believe you might have a message for me, Mrs Hoskins?" She raised her voice only slightly. Probably Amanda would have lost sight of the time. Time didn't mean a thing to her friend.

Mrs Hoskins took heed of the tone. She continued on to where Carol was seated. "The police are at the gate. They want to come in."

Carol's lovely skin blanched. She stared back at the housekeeper, panic rising. "Well, what are you waiting for, Mrs Hoskins? Let them in." Carol's eyes flashed to Damon's. "Something is wrong. They could have had an accident."

"Let's wait and see." Damon rose to his feet, pulling Carol's chair back with one hand. "We'll see to this, Maurice." He looked towards Carol's uncle, who hadn't made a move. Neither had Dallas, who nevertheless had gone extremely pale. So she had some heart after all.

"I do hope everything is okay." Maurice Chancellor spoke earnestly, at the same time lifting his wineglass to his mouth. Dallas continued to sit like a monument made out of granite.

* * *

It was as they had thought. The police gave them a full account: Carol's car was as good as totalled. Neither of them paid heed to that. People counted; cars could be replaced. The young women—the driver and her female passenger—had been taken by ambulance to the district hospital. They had been in a deep state of shock, blood pressure up because of it, but both were conscious, if fuzzy. They had been checked over by paramedics. Mercifully their necks, backs and sternums had not received injury. Probably there was bruising. They would know more once the victims were safely in hospital. The young women could be airlifted to Sydney, if their injuries proved more serious than at first thought.

Both young women had been wearing their seat belts in the correct position, the police told them. Both airbags had been deployed, functioning just as the manufacturer had intended. It appeared the car had taken the worst hit. It had ploughed into a tree at the bottom of a windy downhill stretch of road. The cause of the accident wasn't known. No other vehicle had been involved. There had been no smell of alcohol on either girl's breath or clothing. There had been a delay because most people were at home for Christmas and the wreck had not been spotted until some time later.

"I have to go to them. You'll come with me, Damon?"

"Or course." He rested his hand on the fine-boned curve of her shoulder, wondering what possible explanation there could be for the accident. He just couldn't see Amanda losing control of the car. He couldn't really see her speeding either, although he thought her very impulsive. Something must have gone badly wrong.

But what? The girls were very lucky they had done the right thing, strapping themselves in. He had known of horrific cases brought about by the non-use of seat belts, defective airbags or both.

* * *

In the coming week all was revealed. The brakes of Carol's car had been tampered with. They hadn't got very far into their journey to the nearest town. The reason for the "accident"—no accident at all—had been quickly established: the brake-fluid hose had been injected with water. The girls hadn't travelled many miles because when the brake fluid heated it had turned to gas. As Amanda hit the brakes harder and harder, the gas would have compressed.

"I did the only thing I could," Amanda told them later from her hospital bed. "The car held the road, but I had to make a quick decision. I drove into a tree. Not a *big* one. Just enough to stop us. Both of us were braced. The airbags did the rest."

Enormously relieved for all their sakes, Carol offered the girls a holiday in the Whitsundays, all expenses paid.

"Damn nearly worth it!" Amanda crowed.

Summer was not so sure, but she wasn't about to knock back a free holiday in a luxury hotel in one of the most beautiful parts of the world.

Amanda and Summer were interviewed by the police. Satisfied with their statements, the police let them go off on their travels. The police investigation had come up with the theory that it wasn't Amanda or Summer who had been the target. It was Carol Chancellor, the heiress.

"Who do you think might want to kill you, Ms Chancellor?"

Carol shuddered every time she considered the question, which was many times a day. Everyone at Beaumont had been questioned. Dallas had worked herself up into apoplexy. "How dare anyone suggest I would know anything of it?"

"Whoever it is, he's a psychopath," Damon had reasoned.

"Why's it got to be a *he?*" Carol hazarded a guess.

"Got to be a he, wouldn't you think? Most women know little about the mechanics of cars. It wouldn't have been terribly clever for either your uncle or Troy to try such a thing.

Dallas saw Troy off, I believe, so she was with him. No motive whatever for the guests. It had to be someone who broke in. Remember I spoke about updating security? There were obvious places where someone could get into the grounds."

"Someone *did*."

"Someone who knew you were spending Christmas at Beaumont."

"Maybe my mother's a likely suspect." Carol made the sick joke.

"Highly unlikely," Damon said. "She would have absolutely nothing to gain. And she *is* your mother."

"And she would never get her clothes dirty. The police seem to have come to a dead end. They even interviewed Tracey's ex-boyfriend, when you put them on to him. He had an alibi: he was with Tracey. Incredibly, they've moved back in together."

"How does this happen? *Why* does it happen?" Damon asked, not understanding it at all.

"She used to say she loved him. She was terribly upset when he lost his job at the restaurant—his temper, I'd say. She said Tarik was raised to believe it was no big deal hitting a woman in the family. His father beat his mother. He told Tracey that."

"And that wasn't enough to warn her off? Some women must be easy to brainwash."

Carol had to agree. "Tracey always appeared quite normal, but there must be something seriously amiss with her. The funny thing is, I've seen her go out of her way to provoke him. And she did it at the worst possible times. Weird!"

"The police will continue to keep an eye on him," Damon said. "The matter is not closed. I've hired another man, by the way. Whoever did this is known to you, Carol—maybe even to me. They *will* be caught."

But when?

* * *

The weeks passed and no one was caught. Neither did the incident get into the papers; Damon made sure of that. He had done everything he could do to protect Carol, all too aware her great inheritance had only brought danger into her life. So all the while he was on high alert, as were the bodyguards who continued to shadow her. One private investigator had been given the exclusive job of following Tracey's boyfriend. The agency had an excellent reputation. He knew Carol had her fears but she didn't speak about them. She went about business in a highly professional way. He was proud of her.

He drove her to and fro; she hadn't wanted a new car. He knew the whole incident weighed heavily on her. And him. If anyone decided to attack Carol, they would have to attack him first.

Information came to him all the time. He made sure Carol wasn't trapped in her apartment. As the Chancellor heiress, she was now being invited everywhere, as was he. He knew people were talking, but he couldn't help that. There was too much at stake. They didn't go to restaurants. Too many people had formed the habit of coming up to their table. He didn't think there was any danger at functions where many people were gathered. No one could attack Carol and hope to get away.

Unless they were certifiably mad.

With February came the return to university. This was her final year, a big year. Sometimes she sighted Gary Prescott leaving the building as she came out of the lift. He had stopped leaving messages for her, accepting the fact she had little intention of taking up his invitations. In another lifetime, she might have had coffee with him. But her present life had changed to the extent she had a driver to take her to and from classes. It was all a bit much, but Damon considered it necessary. And there was no use complaining.

A few days later she rode down in the lift with Gary. She had a class that morning at the St James campus in the centre of Sydney's legal and business district. Nearly all her classes were held not at the central location but at the new law school building at Camperdown, opened by the Governor General of Australia, Quentin Bryce, in 2009.

"I guess you know Dad has gone back to Mum," Gary told her with some satisfaction. "I have the use of the penthouse until he sells it. *If* he sells it. For all I know, Dad could run off the rails again."

"I sincerely hope he doesn't, Gary." She studied his face. "It upsets you, doesn't it?"

"Mum is so good."

"I'm sure your father realises that."

"I hope so."

The lift door opened and they stepped out into the foyer. "What's with the driver?" he asked. "I see him there all the time. Can't you drive yourself to uni?"

"Accident to my car," she said briefly.

"Troy never told me that."

She stopped in her tracks. "You know my cousin?"

"Of course I know him. We went to uni together. Can't say he's a friend of mine, but I know him. I run into him now and again. He reckons that lawyer guy of yours is making a big play for you."

Carol gave a definite sigh. "That's the story he's putting around. It's not true, Gary. I'd appreciate it if you'd quash the rumour. Damon Hunter is a man of integrity."

She spoke so forcefully, Gary laughingly backed off. "Okay, I believe you. Never liked your cousin anyway. Hear he got the big bucks—he's more up himself than ever. He'll get more when his mother kicks the bucket. She got plenty from her old man."

Carol looked surprised. She knew little about Dallas's family.

"Surely you know Barney Lebermann was her old man?" Gary stood looking down at her.

"Well, yes, I did know her maiden name was Lebermann."

"The country's biggest luxury car dealer," Gary said. "Centurion bought him out years ago. The guy had a whole collection of vintage vehicles. He collected them like works of art. All European—even had an old London taxi. Not a lot of people knew about his collection. My dad did—he's a car enthusiast. Troy's mother used to drive a very nice Italian sports car when she was young. Used to look after it herself, according to Troy, if you could ever believe him."

That struck a dismal chord. "Well, that's something I never knew. I was estranged from the family from age five."

"But you're back together again now?"

"In a manner of speaking," Carol said. "Can I give you a lift anywhere, Gary? I'm going into the CBD—class at the St James campus."

"That'd suit me fine. Dad told me to show up early. This is as early as it gets. I'm working for him, you know."

Class over, Carol rang her driver to let him know. He told her to wait outside the Philip Street entrance. He was only five or six minutes away. Carol caught up with two of her fellow students who fired off a couple of questions. Everyone knew Carol Chancellor was *very* smart and she could always be relied upon to clarify difficult points in their lectures.

Outside the front of the building on her own, Carol saw a taxi drop off a passenger. It was Tracey. She hadn't heard a word from Tracey over the last month or so. In short, having gone back to Tarik, Tracey had cut herself off from her friends who had so disapproved of him. There was no doubt in Carol's mind that she had to speak to her.

She moved forward as the taxi moved off. "Trace?"

There was a moment when it looked like Tracey was about to bolt.

"Please, Tracey, a word. I won't keep you."

"I know, I know. I should have got in touch with you, Carol." Tracey's embarrassment was evident. "You were always so nice to me. So kind and supportive."

"But you're back with Tarik now?"

Tracey cast her eyes onto the pavement. "He's so sorry for what he did. We're having counselling. He hasn't laid a finger on me—I've told him I'll leave him for good if he does."

"And will you?" Carol asked gravely.

"I really believe he's going to change. You look so beautiful, Caro. I've missed you. I want you to know Tarik had nothing to do with that accident the police spoke to us about. He was with me."

"All the time?"

"All the time," Tracey said, not defensively, but most emphatically. "Tarik wouldn't dare to hurt my friends. He's all talk. He knows what would happen to him if he did. We were nowhere near your grandfather's country house—I mean *your* country house. We were in Sydney the whole time. I swear to you, Caro, Tarik is a changed man. I'm pregnant."

Oh, God! "Tracey!" Carol said, leaning forward to give her old friend a big hug. "You don't show."

"Only just found out. Tarik is thrilled out of his mind. Look, it's lovely to see you, but I must fly. I have an appointment."

"I'm here if you need me, Tracey," Carol said. She didn't trust Tarik so she didn't give out her phone numbers. "Damon Hunter is my go-between. He will let me know."

"I'm fine, Caro. Honestly. You take good care of yourself."

"You, too, Trace."

Tracey sped off. Carol knew she was unlikely to hear from Tracey again. Tarik controlled her. At the same time, would Tracey lie for him, given her old friend Amanda could have been killed? Hard to tell.

CHAPTER EIGHT

IT WAS WELL after six before Damon could leave the office. Carol had rung him saying she had some news and could he call in at her apartment. Emotion had coloured her voice. He had asked her what she'd found out, but she wouldn't tell him, saying she didn't want to speak on the phone.

"Just come if you can."

"I'll be there."

He would always be there for her. It was as simple and as difficult as that. He had come to accept he would go to hell and back to keep Carol Chancellor safe.

"Hi," she said, looking up at him. The irises of her eyes were the most intense blue.

He bent his head to brush her petal-soft cheek. A lovely rose scent came from her skin and her hair. "So what's up?" It was all he could do not to sweep her into his arms. Surely the control he continued to exert was a powerful gauge of his love? He was madly in love for the first time in his life. It was an extraordinary sensation, not being able to give in completely to his deepest desires. But there was such a thing as a code of conduct.

"Come into the living room," she invited. "Would you like a drink?"

"A shot of whisky would be good. It's been a long day."

"Let me get it for you." She moved off in her graceful way.

"How's everything going?" He took off his jacket.

"I'm working hard, Damon. I won't let you down."

"I didn't mean that. How *are* you?"

"A bit different from yesterday." She came back with his drink. She was wearing indigo-blue cotton denim jeans with a sleeveless hot-pink shirt that, far from clashing with her hair, made a fine colour contrast. She took the sofa opposite him as though she, too, was trying to adhere to a code of conduct.

He took a gulp of the single-malt Scotch. "I'm all attention."

"I could be making a lot out of nothing."

"Not you, Carol. Anyway, let me be the judge of that."

"Okay." Carol launched into the events of the day: her meetings with Gary Prescott and the accidental meeting with her old friend Tracey, now pregnant to her formerly abusive lover. Tarik, according to Tracey, was a changed man.

Could a leopard change its spots?

Damon listened without once interrupting. "Let's not rush to judgement. But your uncle knew all this without saying a word."

"I think Dallas has some power over him."

"That could well be. He certainly doesn't love her. Maybe staying with her is a form of self-preservation. Dallas probably shared her father's passion for cars. She lived in the world of cars, luxury cars. I don't know whether she would be capable of servicing a sports car. I think not, but she'd know a lot. She'd know how to disable a car. Any car."

"Do we really think she'd be capable of trying to injure, even kill me? That's a giant leap."

"It sure is."

She could see how intent he was. "Has she gone mad, for God's sake?"

"She might feel she had enormous provocation. She's lost too much over the years. She lost her husband along the way, unfaithful to her with your mother. One can't discount naked jealousy. Then there's the fact she no more wants to leave Beaumont than your uncle. She knows you are going to ask them to leave eventually. In her eyes, you humiliated her son. Your mother humiliated her. There's a sick reasoning to it—enough to suspect her, anyway. When the police questioned her, you would have thought she didn't know one end of a car from the other."

"I supposed Uncle Maurice always did the driving. Stupid of me. If she tampered with the brakes of my car, she has to be stark-raving bonkers. I mean, what's she going to do next, wave a gun at me? Get someone else to do it? She was going out on the shoot, you know. Uncle Maurice is the country squire and she's the lady of the manor. In a way, she's a whole lot tougher than my mother. Uncle Maurice truly doesn't believe Roxanne had anything to do with my father's accident."

"But he backed Dallas in order to survive. There has to be something she has on him worth investigating. Maybe a spot of embezzling? I wouldn't be unduly surprised."

"Maybe Uncle Maurice never thought for a moment she would deliberately sabotage the brakes?"

"She had motive. She had opportunity. You had garaged your car. Troy took his own car. He left early. His mother saw him off. It's very plausible."

"And simply too dreadful if it's true. Amanda and Summer could have been badly injured, even killed. No wonder she went as white as a sheet when the police arrived. I thought she was showing a bit of heart."

"Well, *you* were the target, not your friends."

"So what do we do with this? Leave it alone?"

"All actions have consequences, Carol."

"Can you imagine what a scandal it would create if we pointed the finger at Dallas?"

"People love scandals, especially among the rich." Damon masked his deep concern with sarcasm.

"Do you think Troy would have stepped back and let me die?" she asked in horror.

"Do you think he could have helped his mother?" The very thought robbed her of breath.

"No, I don't." Damon had already arrived at his conclusion. "Troy might be a lightweight with too much money for his own good, but he's leading a fairly normal life. He's so arrogant he had thought it could include you. He isn't after the money or the huge responsibilities. He would find them an enormous burden. He had hopes for the two of you. You successfully crushed them. He'd be angry and mortified but he'd eventually shrug it off. Make a future joke of it. Can't you see him?"

In a way she could. "How can anyone know? Barely six months have gone by since my grandfather died and someone is trying to get me out of the way. What do they *want?* Was it *wrong* for my grandfather to make me his heir? Didn't he consider for a moment he could be putting me in danger? He *knew* his family. He *knew* Dallas."

"He may have had little time for them, Carol, but I'm certain he didn't see them as potential murderers." Damon tried to calm her.

"He had no trouble believing it of my mother," she said bitterly.

"Carol, Selwyn Chancellor lost his adored son and heir. Your grandmother, Elaine, lost her son. They said the things they did because they were off their heads with grief. They were looking for a culprit. Roxanne fitted the bill."

"Well, she wasn't exactly squeaky clean, was she?" Carol said dismally. "Two brothers shared her. At least we now know Adam was my father." DNA tests had been conducted and the results delivered. Carol had avoided telling her mother, not actually believing her mother would care.

"All we have is circumstantial evidence. No proof. I could confront Dallas," he suggested, wanting to spare Carol further trauma.

"*We* can confront her," Carol said. "She's not innocent."

Damon shook his head. "We don't know that, Carol. Tracey could well be covering for the father of her coming child. If she's crazy enough to go back to her abuser, to allow herself to fall pregnant to him, we have to assume she's capable of lying for him, as well."

"Let's start on Dallas first." Carol felt suddenly beyond fear. She had Damon on her side. Who else did she need?

They left their visit to the following Saturday. Carol informed her uncle she would be coming. She didn't say why; for all she knew, Dallas could arm herself with a weapon.

"There comes a time to confront people," Carol said determinedly as the massive gates to Beaumont opened.

She didn't sound angry or afraid. She sounded ready to go into battle. "Allow the possibility we could be wrong, Carol," Damon warned.

"Only we're *not* wrong."

Maurice Chancellor himself greeted them at the door. "This is a pleasant surprise. Come in. Come in. You're staying for the weekend, I hope?"

"Just today, Uncle Maurice, as I said."

"Mrs Chancellor at home?" Damon asked, raising his glance to the gallery.

"As a matter of fact, she's not. She's visiting a friend."

"Might I suggest you ring her and get her to come back home?" Damon said. "Where exactly does her friend live?"

Maurice looked from one to the other. "Is anything wrong?

You've found out something about the accident? You could have told me on the phone. We were terribly anxious."

Carol thought it was going to get a whole lot worse before it got better. "So, how far away is Dallas? Please don't tell me Hong Kong."

Maurice Chancellor flushed. "My dear girl, she's down the road. *Mayfair*—you would have passed it. Not that you can see the house from the road. But come in, come in. You'd like coffee, I expect?"

"Thank you, Uncle Maurice," Carol said. "I'll go through to the kitchen while you ring Dallas. It's most important she be here."

Maurice knitted his brows. "What for? Dallas knows nothing."

"About what, sir?" Damon intervened. "We haven't said why we want to speak to you both."

"*We* now, is it?" Maurice looked more accepting than disapproving.

"I am Carol's lawyer and advisor," Damon pointed out smoothly. "It was your father's wish."

"Of course it was. I'll ring Dallas from the study." He made off.

He must have had some difficulty persuading his wife to return because when they saw him again, his colour was high and he looked thoroughly rattled.

"Didn't want to come?" Carol asked.

"Isn't that the truth," he responded wryly. "A very tough lady, is my wife."

"What's she got on you, Uncle Maurice? We know it's something."

The wryness shifted to extreme nervousness. "I don't know what you're talking about, Carol."

Damon cut in. "You're being given the opportunity, sir, to

come clean. If Dallas weren't your wife, one might suspect her of blackmailing you into staying in a loveless marriage."

Maurice Chancellor looked so badly shocked he might have been shot in the heart. "She could ruin me. It was in the early days of our marriage. My father was withholding money from me. He was always intent on pointing out how ineffective I was. Adam was the great hero, the son made in his own corporate image. I freely admit I'm no great shakes when it comes to business, but I managed to siphon off quite a few million. I was fool enough to tell Dallas. In the early days, she went through quite a lot of money, believe it or not. She always had to have a high-end luxury car. Of course, her father at the time was one of the country's luxury car dealers."

"And she threatened to go to your father when you became involved with my mother?" Carol asked.

"Exactly." Maurice Chancellor hung his head. He looked wretched. "I'll pay it all back, Carol. At least my father left me a rich man."

"I have just the charity you can donate it to," Carol flashed back. "How many million was it, Uncle Maurice? I dare say we can find out."

Dallas Chancellor arrived thirty minutes later, half circling the drive fast and braking right at the foot of the stone steps. To say she looked furious wouldn't adequately describe it. Dallas Chancellor had little difficulty working herself into a volcanic rage.

"What is this all about?" She stared around the group with over-bright, steely-grey eyes. They had finished coffee and were sitting quietly waiting for her.

"A chat," Damon said. "Won't you sit down, Mrs Chancellor?"

It said a lot for his natural authority that she did just that.

"Now, are you going to tell me what's so important it couldn't keep?" She plonked herself down heavily into an armchair.

"The little matter of the car crash," Damon said as though it was nothing to worry about. "We all know it wasn't an accident. When the police questioned you, Mrs Chancellor, you acted outraged. It was a fine performance. You never said you knew a great deal about cars."

"So what?" Dallas shot back. "It was irrelevant."

"No, it was you concealing a significant fact." His tone firmed. "The fact you know cars could explain what might have happened. On your own admission, you hate Carol's mother."

"Positively *loathe* her," Dallas confirmed.

"We all know that. A couple of days ago, Carol ran into someone who told her all about your father and his collection of vintage cars. From all accounts, you loved cars as much as your father. You favoured an Italian make, I believe?"

"So what?" Dallas repeated as though she could keep it up forever.

Maurice Chancellor picked up a silver pot on a silver tray and poured himself some cold coffee.

"We're hoping you'll tell us what you're trying to hide." Carol forgot Damon's lawyerly words of caution. "It was you who tampered with the brakes of my car. You had the opportunity when you saw Troy off. You had the necessary skill."

Two things happened. Dallas laughed and the coffee cup fell out of Maurice Chancellor's nerveless hand onto the beautiful rug. "God! Say something, Dallas," he begged. "This can't possibly be true. It's that Tarik fella. The police thought so, though they mightn't be able to pin it on him with his trumped-up alibi."

"Of course it is!" was Dallas's swift reply. "You've put two and two together, Carol, my dear, and come up with ten."

Damon's expression turned severely judicial. "We are,

however, going to the police with what we've learned, Mrs Chancellor. There's a tremendous amount of hate in you. All those years of jealousy deepened and darkened. The police are not in possession of the true facts. They saw you as a rich woman who genuinely knows nothing about the mechanics of cars. They'll have a fine time chewing over what we've since discovered. They'll have questions. They'll expect you to come up with the right answers."

"Except you *can't,* can you?" Carol felt pressure behind her eyes, tried to blink it away.

Cold coffee was seeping into the valuable rug but no one paid any attention. Maurice Chancellor sat back, staring around so woozily he could have been drunk.

"I saw Troy off then I went back upstairs *immediately,*" Dallas announced in her best 'lady of the manor' voice. "My husband will confirm that," she added with utter confidence.

"Well, Uncle Maurice?" Carol asked, trying hard to control her distress. It was so difficult to be strong.

"I can assure you, I won't let you get away with slandering me," Dallas threatened, fully prepared to brazen it out. 'Well, Maurice, don't just sit there gawping."

Maurice Chancellor's belated response was to rise to his feet. "Why don't we call the police now?" he said, moving to stand directly in front of his wife. "You didn't return to our bedroom, Dallas, after you saw Troy off. It was a good while after. I intend to tell the police that."

"Will you, now?" Dallas gave a loud, trumpeting laugh full of contempt. "I'll have something to tell them, as well."

"Don't bother," Maurice said in the voice of self-loathing. "Carol and Damon already know. I've made my confession. You were an accessory to embezzlement, by the way. Ponder that. You've held it over me for many long, unhappy years. What a gutless creature I am. You've ruined our son, by the way. Carol is allowing me to pay the money into one of her charities. I'll be more than happy to do that."

Dallas, too, was on her feet, showing the tremendous weight of anger in her. "You fool!"

Maurice Chancellor's handsome face was full of desolation. "The biggest mistake of my life was picking you for my wife. You were never the person I thought you were. No wonder I fell in love with Roxanne. I got little of it from you, or anyone else, for that matter. I was the forgotten boy, the forgotten man. I was never *real* to anyone. Not even my mother."

"Who was a basket case!"

"You're *real* to me, Uncle Maurice," Carol said, suddenly feeling very sorry for him. "Please sit down again. We have to work out what to do." Her blue gaze was more sad than recriminatory.

"Thank you for that, Carol," he said with a bent head.

Ninety minutes later, they were back in Sydney. Both of them had been very quiet in the car, both shaken by Dallas's total lack of repentance. She had admitted nothing, but they just knew she was guilty. How to prove it? How to avoid a terrible scandal? How was it to be dealt with? Yet another terrible family secret? There could be no miraculous reconciliation; that was out of the question. Was Dallas still to be feared? The extraordinary thing was, Maurice Chancellor was all for keeping it in the family.

"Dallas can clear off. Get out of the country," he had said by way of a solution. "Believe me, she wouldn't fancy going to jail."

The city, so beautiful by day with its magnificent blue harbour, was dazzling by night. The city towers and the icons, the Opera House and the Harbour Bridge, were ablaze with lights. For once Carol couldn't find her usual response of delight in the sight. Damon saw her to her apartment. She stood quietly inside the door for a moment, looking a little bereft. She held her hands to her temples, then rubbed them. "Headache." It couldn't be her voice. It sounded so young. "Come in, Damon. Please don't run away." It was Saturday night. He could be going somewhere, when she badly wanted him beside her. She was sick of their set of rules.

"I've no intention of going anywhere, Carol. I'm not surprised you've got a headache. You're in shock."

"Plus the fact I haven't been sleeping. Dallas tried to kill me, Damon." She turned to him in utter disbelief. "Her mission failed. I wasn't driving my car. But it was a miracle Amanda and Summer escaped with little injury. What's to stop Dallas from trying again? She's challenging us to go to the police—circumstantial evidence, no witnesses to what we say she did. Troy would back her. Dallas said my grandmother was a basket case. What does she think *she* is? I'll tell you what she is—she's deranged. I'm just so grateful she's not my blood."

Damon looked grim. "Let's not think about that now. I'll get you a couple of painkillers. Where are they?"

"In one of the kitchen drawers. Could you make me a cup of coffee—no, *tea*—as soon as possible, Damon?" she asked in a shaky voice.

"Migraine? I know they can be really bad."

"I don't suffer from migraines. Just a pounding here near my temples." She placed her fingers against the spots. "I'll take this outfit off, find something…" Her voice trailed off. "You know where things are."

"Leave it to me."

When she returned she was wearing a long, floaty garment held by a halter around the neck. The fabric was lovely, silk on a sapphire-blue ground patterned in swirls of darker blue and green with touches of gold. He held the glass of water out to her, with two painkillers.

"Thank you, Damon. You didn't have plans for tonight, did you?"

"Swallow the tablets," he said, waiting until she had done so before taking the glass off her. "Sit down on the sofa and try to relax."

"So much bad history in my family," she lamented, moving off slowly. "Now this. She wasn't exactly drowning in guilt, was she? Maybe her sanity has gone."

"Sit quietly, Carol. Find an area of peace," he advised.

"Come and sit beside me, if you're not planning to go away." She felt reduced to pleading. "You're always holding yourself in check. You think we went too far, too fast, don't you?" She stared up at him, trying to read his closed expression, unreadable to her.

"I won't come and sit beside you until you stop talking," Damon said. "Give the painkillers time to work."

"That could be ten minutes." She was quiet for a moment, before firing up again. "What did she expect me to say? All is forgiven? God!" She met his dark eyes. "Okay, okay. I just need you beside me. I'll close my eyes."

"Good girl."

"I'm a *woman,* Damon, with a woman's needs."

As though she had to remind him! Every nerve in his body was strung tight.

"I feel a bit sick," she said after a few moments.

"Breathe," he urged very gently, putting a cradling arm around her. He couldn't do otherwise. The scent of crushed rose petals floated from her skin, intoxicating him. "Keep breathing."

She tried to give herself up to it.

"Keep going," he murmured. "One breath after an-

other. You…can…feel…your…tension…going. Breathe…
breathe…" He spaced out the words.

Carol rested her head against his shoulder feeling a rush of
peace. "I'm so tired," she murmured. Her heartbeat slowed,
her breathing began to even out.

"Then sleep," Damon bid her. "I'm here."

"That's all that matters," she said drowsily, already beginning to drift away. Damon had the most wonderful soothing
voice. Carol curled herself around him like a drowsy, con-
tented cat.

How difficult that made it to control the molten rush of
blood through his veins. She was so small against him, but it
was a woman's body she possessed, effortlessly, innocently
seductive. He could feel her warmth through the fabric of her
floaty dress that showed off an unrestrained outline of her
small, perfect breasts. He rested his chin in her rosy curls.
Her breathing had deepened. She was in a light sleep when
his strong male body was racked with sensations as painful
as they were exquisite. How was he expected to endure this?

Make the effort, his inner voice countered sternly. *If she
means so much to you, you can do it. Think of it as a test of
your resolve to do what is best for her.*

He began to count, anything to suppress the build-up of
sexual excitement. One… He counted four seconds before
two… Four seconds before three… And so on. It wasn't all
that easy to keep the count without concentrating on what he
was doing. Heaven would surely reward his efforts.

He must have dozed off himself because when he opened his
eyes and looked down at her she was staring up at him, her
eyes a fabulous blue.

"The headache's gone," she whispered.

"I'm glad."

She kept staring at him, her porcelain skin lightly flushed, her lovely mouth parted, showing the tips of her small white teeth.

He could feel himself unravelling. She looked heartbreakingly young. "What are you trying to do to me, Carol? Whatever it is, I don't know that I can combat it."

"Hush now." She placed two fingers against his mouth. "Listen to your own heart."

"I'm trying to listen to my head."

"Sometimes the heart has more power than the head. Kiss me, Damon," she invited softly. "I *need* you to kiss me. I know you want to."

His tone was harsh, even to his own ears. "Carol, you know very well it won't end there."

Every word of rejection hurt her. "What's the point of this stand-off, Damon?" she burst out in utter frustration. "You act as though I'm under-age. You act as though making love to me will break all the rules of good conduct. You act like you *wrote* the damned things."

"Some things are set in stone." He thrust a hand through his thick coal-black hair. "You're very vulnerable at this point, Carol. You've had a bad shock. You're off-balance."

"So you're telling me I shouldn't be here in your arms?" She sank into sarcasm.

"Carol, baby, please."

She half sat up. "I refuse to be shut out," she told him fiercely. "I *love* you. Love you. Love you. Love you. You've got a big problem with that?" Her voice rose and echoed.

He caught her wrists, his emotions dangerously unchained by her passionate admission. That gave him far too much power. "Don't you know—?" he cried.

The rest of the sentence remained unspoken. "Don't underestimate me, Damon. I know it all."

She was looking back at him as though they were at war. "Carol, you're my responsibility. It's my duty—"

"Oh, shut up about your sacred duty." The speed with which they had come to clashing was dazzling. She struck him again, feeling his chest muscles tighten against the attack.

He tried to joke. "Those sessions at the gym have to stop."

"Don't!" Suddenly she snapped. She made a violent move to get away from him, in the process winding her long dress mummylike around her body. Instead of managing a leap to her feet, she almost took a tumble.

He caught her back to him, incredible tension in his hard, throbbing body. The emotional temperature was going through the roof. Even the air around them crackled with charge. His feelings for her forced him to take a fantastic turn around. Hunger for her grew stronger than his resolve. His body knew him better than he knew himself. He started to kiss her, his hand snaking into her silky curls so she couldn't turn her head. He was kissing her not like she was a precious piece of porcelain but a living, breathing *woman,* a woman he desired above all others. He had urged her earlier to breathe in and out to calm herself, only he was kissing her so passionately she might scarcely be able to breathe at all.

He lifted his mouth fractionally from hers, only she whispered fiercely, "Don't you dare stop."

"As unlikely as that appears to be. But understand, I will reach a point when I won't be able to stop." He gave fair warning.

"You think I don't know that?" She stared up at him incredulously. "Keep going, Damon. I *mean* it. I'm tired of obeying the rules. Make love to me. If you don't, I promise you, I'll simply crack up."

"Don't I know the way that works?" he said with black humour, his resonant voice slipping deep in his throat. Control had moved off a great distance. It was a frenzy of longing she aroused in him, the craving to have her. Heiress or not, he wouldn't give her up. Not after she had told him she loved him. Over and over. For that he was willing to pay any price.

Wall sconces glimmered along the hallway. He lifted her in his arms with great ease, carrying her down the corridor and setting her on her bed. The skirt of her lovely dress belled out around her. To him she was the most desirable woman in the world.

"Well, here we are, Carol!" He bent over her, his breathing coming hard. "This is decision time. You have to be absolutely sure."

For an answer she knelt up on the bed, bouncing a little on the springy mattress but still managing to get a grip on him. "Come here to me, you gorgeous man." She allowed herself to fall back, pulling his upper body down over her, revelling in the weight of it against her breasts. "It's okay, Damon," she whispered, her eyes on the moulded arabesques on the plastered ceiling. "You won't make me pregnant. Not tonight, anyway. I'm on the pill. All for you," she added. "Let me make that plain."

He was astonished and aroused. "You *meant* for me to make love to you, you wicked girl?"

She offered a laugh that entranced him. "God, Damon, I've lived for this moment. You've changed my world. Don't you know that? Everything has become more meaningful. I know you want me. I suppose it's possible I might want you more, but—"

She got no further. "I'll show you *want*." He placed one hand over her breast, feeling the tightly budded nipple. "You're more precious to me than an Aladdin's cave full of treasure—chests brimming over with diamonds, rubies, emeralds, sapphires like your eyes." He lifted his head a moment, as though struck by a thought. "Actually, I *love* rubies. What about you?"

"My favourite gemstone!" Carol cried, her whole being exuding joy. "Come back here to me."

"I can, now *that's* out of the way." He lowered his head to kiss her, feeling her gently slide the tip of her tongue into his mouth.

"What's out of the way?" she asked after some time.

"Never you mind." His voice was faintly slurred. He had a ruby engagement ring in mind. Slowly he began to undo the halter that held her dress. "How should I describe you, *my* little seductress?"

She gave him a slow, sweet, incandescent smile. "My philosophy is, if offered a heaven-sent opportunity, one should never turn it down. However, apart from telling me I'm more valuable to you than a treasure trove of precious jewels, you haven't yet told me you *love* me."

"How could I not?" The expression on his handsome face turned very serious. "To love you is my fate. I loved you from the moment I laid eyes on you—the adorable little redhead, so full of fight. I intend to tell you just how much I love you right through the night."

"I can't ask for more than that."

"I'll never run out of love for you." He looked deeply into her eyes.

"Nor I for you." Carol lifted her mouth to give him a kiss that was hot, sweet and fierce.

The intimacy between them seemed to Damon like the greatest gift life could afford. Very slowly, he began to peel her dress down to her hips. Her skin was flawless in the lamplight, her naked breasts small, high, perfect, inviting his mouth and his hands. He bent his head and pressed his open mouth against one tight pink bud, catching one nipple then the other very gently with his teeth. "Are you a virgin?" he asked very quietly.

She lay back, her body consumed by sensation. "I know

you aren't, but I am. I'm one of the very few around. So, now you know you're going to transform me. Maiden into woman. I never got past petting, Damon. You will be my *first* lover." She felt exultant now. "Does that worry you?" She reached out to him as he pondered her question.

Damon had to consider how the strength of his feelings, the power of his body, his driving male need for her, might impact on her. He wanted to give her only *pleasure*.

"Not at all," he said after a moment, the strength of his love for her showing in his eyes. "I'll take it very, *very* slowly. I want this to be one of the all-time memorable experiences of our lives."

She was so moved she could scarcely speak. "So it's til death do us part?" Tears glittered in her eyes.

"Yes, Carol, my love, it is." He said it like a sacred vow, which indeed was what he felt.

"And it's a yes for me, too." Carol's voice matched his intensity. "You're my fixed star, Damon. I need you. I'll always need you."

"And I'll always be there for you." He raised her slender arm, kissing the length of it, from her wrist to her elbow to the curve of her shoulder. "Marry me," he begged, his dark eyes brilliant with love and pride in her. "It will be a communion of our bodies and our souls."

"The way it should be if one is blessed." There was no question of pausing for Carol, not even for a second. Her face took on a very special radiance. "I'll be *everything* you want."

"But you are already." Damon dipped his head to kiss the soft hollow of her throat.

High emotion assailed them. Carol pressed her palms hard against the coverlet, half-faint with wanting. "So, a night to remember?" She gazed up at him with blue smouldering eyes.

"Let me show you what love is," he resolved, smiling into her eyes.

"Then I want you to start. *Right now.*"

It was miraculous and it was simple: total commitment made manifest.

In such a world as Damon and Carol were destined to live in, neither as it turned out could have hoped for a more perfect partner or a more perfect ally. The one was always there for the other. That alone conferred tremendous strength on a union that was further blessed with children, boy and girl, who would be given all the love, the support, the trust, and the training to carve their own successful paths in life.

EPILOGUE

CAROL AND DAMON had recently returned from their honeymoon when Maurice Chancellor rang to ask if he could call in. He was told, *of course*. Maurice was still living at Beaumont, writing his magnum opus, a crime novel of memories and murder. It was by all accounts going well. He had a publisher and an excellent editor who gave him many a helpful suggestion and lots of encouragement.

Divorce proceedings were well under way. In less than a year and a day, Maurice Chancellor and his wife Dallas would enter a new phase in life. Dallas in fact had already entered one. She had chosen to live in London. Though strictly speaking she hadn't been left with a choice, just a clear directive. She had been told never to return.

Were it not for his overly careful movements, Carol wouldn't have thought anything was amiss. But something definitely was. She braced herself. She and Damon were sublimely happy, working as a finely meshed team. She had graduated in law with first-class honours. Christmas was coming up, a wonderful time of the year that they would share together. They were so enjoying their lives and one another, full of their hopes and plans.

Maurice waited until they were all seated in the living room of their new penthouse apartment, a fresh start. The Chancellor mansion on the harbour had sold within a week of its going on the market. Carol and Damon had the proceeds of the sale earmarked for medical research into childhood autism and programmes to significantly brighten future prospects for children with the disorder and the lives of the caring parents.

"So what is it, Uncle Maurice?" Carol asked. She and her uncle had grown much closer. He had, in fact, given her away at the wedding—the wedding of the year, and no mistake! It had been an unforgettable day for everyone. Roxanne, looking marvellous, had even shed a few motherly tears. There had been no jocular mention of when she might expect her first grandchild. Roxanne probably couldn't survive being a grandmother.

"There's some news…" Maurice said and let the sentence trail.

"Please tell us," Carol prompted.

He spread his hands. "I must be a terribly cold-hearted man, but I can't feel any sort of grief. I *want* to, but I can't. I'm just numb." In truth, he had been numb since his wife's confession to tampering with Carol's car before she had left for London. Shockingly, she had shown little in the way of remorse.

Damon reached for his wife's hand, as ever highly protective of her well-being. On her left hand Carol wore her engagement ring above her diamond-banded wedding ring. He had asked the city's top jeweller to hand-make the ring using the finest Burmese ruby the jeweller could source. He had designed the ring himself, an oval 3.59 ruby, the gemstone associated with love and passion banded by baguette diamonds to match Carol's wedding ring.

Maurice's voice brought him out of his moment of reverie. "It's Dallas," he said heavily. "Her luck has finally run out. She was involved in a pile up on the M1. Weather conditions were very bad. She was travelling too fast, couldn't stop."

Something shifted inside Carol. "You're saying she didn't survive the crash?" She was unable to prevent a moment's relief before dismay prevailed. Death was death, but she still had the occasional nightmare about Dallas and her plans.

"She didn't." Maurice replied, a mix of emotions engraved on his handsome face. "Troy is knocked sideways. He's going over there. Put simply, Troy is the only one who loved her. I suppose you'd have to qualify that and say, in his own way. Poor Dallas, she was her own worst enemy," he said like a bone-weary man.

She certainly was, Damon thought, convinced the super-rich thought they were different from everyone else. He drew his beautiful wife, the love of his life, ever closer. "No one wants to hear of a death, Maurice, and the pain it inflicts on those remaining, but whatever happened with Dallas in the past is over. Carol and I—we hope you, too—are looking to the future. Your book is going well, from all accounts. Your editor tells you you've got the talent. You have to take it as far as you can.

"We have some news, too. I was offered a full partnership at Bradfield Douglass. I expected it, but Carol and I have talked it over and we've decided to go out on our own. I always intended to at some stage. Now is the time and I'll have my wife beside me. We'll build our own firm, Hunter Chancellor."

Maurice searched their expressive faces. "Well, that is wonderful to hear. Splendid to bring Carol in."

"She'll be an asset," Damon maintained.

"So I will." Carol turned her head to kiss her husband's cheek.

For the first time Maurice gave a smile. "Perhaps I should start thinking about shifting my allegiance from Marcus Bradfield." Marcus had become too set in his ways, not much thinking outside the box.

"Up to you, Uncle Maurice," Carol said, thinking there was wisdom in such a decision. "My husband is positively brilliant, as Grandfather came to realise. As a family, we've outrun the past, Uncle Maurice. Our future is made every day."

Maurice Chancellor studied his beautiful niece. Would that he had such a daughter! "A long, very happy life to both of you," he said with the utmost sincerity, his battered heart filling with comfort. Perhaps when he got home he would call his son, saying he would join him in London. He had to take better care of his son than his father had ever taken of him. He saw now he had been offered a second chance. How did that make him?

Happy, he realised.

* * * * *

COMING NEXT MONTH from Harlequin® Romance
AVAILABLE APRIL 2, 2013

#4371 SPARKS FLY WITH THE BILLIONAIRE
Marion Lennox

Banker Matthew Bond has to foreclose on a circus. But he hadn't bargained on feisty Allie Miski, who will do anything to protect what is hers.

#4372 A DADDY FOR HER SONS
The Single Mom Diaries
Raye Morgan

Connor McNair never thought he'd get a second chance with Jill Darling. Soon she and her twin babies have him questioning his playboy lifestyle.

#4373 ALONG CAME TWINS...
Tiny Miracles
Rebecca Winters

Kellie Petralia, soon to be ex-wife of Greek billionaire Leandros, is pregnant with twins! Can Leandros convince her their marriage deserves a second chance?

#4374 AN ACCIDENTAL FAMILY
Ami Weaver

Lainey Keeler never thought she'd end up single, pregnant and living on firefighter Ben Lawless's land. But could this be their chance for a family?

You can find more information on upcoming Harlequin® titles, free excerpts and more at www.Harlequin.com.

HRCNM0313

REQUEST YOUR FREE BOOKS!
2 FREE NOVELS PLUS 2 FREE GIFTS!

H HARLEQUIN®

Romance

From the Heart, For the Heart

YES! Please send me 2 FREE Harlequin® Romance novels and my 2 FREE gifts (gifts are worth about $10). After receiving them, if I don't wish to receive any more books, I can return the shipping statement marked "cancel." If I don't cancel, I will receive 6 brand-new novels every month and be billed just $4.09 per book in the U.S. or $4.49 per book in Canada. That's a savings of at least 14% off the cover price! It's quite a bargain! Shipping and handling is just 50¢ per book in the U.S. and 75¢ per book in Canada.* I understand that accepting the 2 free books and gifts places me under no obligation to buy anything. I can always return a shipment and cancel at any time. Even if I never buy another book, the two free books and gifts are mine to keep forever.

114/314 HDN FVR7

Name	(PLEASE PRINT)	
Address		Apt. #
City	State/Prov.	Zip/Postal Code

Signature (if under 18, a parent or guardian must sign)

Mail to the Harlequin® Reader Service:
IN U.S.A.: P.O. Box 1867, Buffalo, NY 14240-1867
IN CANADA: P.O. Box 609, Fort Erie, Ontario L2A 5X3

**Are you a subscriber to Harlequin Romance books
and want to receive the larger-print edition?
Call 1-800-873-8635 or visit www.ReaderService.com.**

* Terms and prices subject to change without notice. Prices do not include applicable taxes. Sales tax applicable in N.Y. Canadian residents will be charged applicable taxes. Offer not valid in Quebec. This offer is limited to one order per household. Not valid for current subscribers to Harlequin Romance books. All orders subject to credit approval. Credit or debit balances in a customer's account(s) may be offset by any other outstanding balance owed by or to the customer. Please allow 4 to 6 weeks for delivery. Offer available while quantities last.

Your Privacy—The Harlequin® Reader Service is committed to protecting your privacy. Our Privacy Policy is available online at www.ReaderService.com or upon request from the Harlequin Reader Service.

We make a portion of our mailing list available to reputable third parties that offer products we believe may interest you. If you prefer that we not exchange your name with third parties, or if you wish to clarify or modify your communication preferences, please visit us at www.ReaderService.com/consumerschoice or write to us at Harlequin Reader Service Preference Service, P.O. Box 9062, Buffalo, NY 14269. Include your complete name and address.

HR13

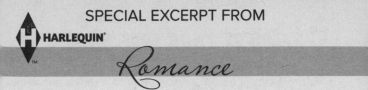
When the bank forecloses on her family circus,
performer Allie Miski will do whatever it takes to save it.
Even if it means working closely with brooding banker
Mathew Bond....

HIS HAND WAS on her shoulder. He could feel her breathing.

She was glaring up at him, breathing too fast. She should break away. He expected her to, but she didn't.

Why? The night held no answer. It was as if they were locked there, motionless in time and space.

One woman and one man...

Her face was just there. Her mouth was just there.

Don't get involved.

How could he not? Something was happening here that was stronger than him. He didn't understand it, but he had no hope of fighting it.

It'd take a stronger man than he was to resist, and he didn't resist.

She didn't move. She stood and looked up at him in the moonlight, anger and despair mixed, but something else... something else...

He didn't understand that look. It was something he had no hope of understanding, and neither, he thought, did she.

Loneliness? Fear? Desperation?

He knew it was none of those things, but maybe it was an emotion born of all three.

It was an emotion he'd never met before, but it was an emotion he couldn't question, for there was no time here or space for asking questions. There was only this woman, looking up at him.

"Allie, I care," he said, and it was as though someone else was talking.

"How can you care?"

He had no answer. He only knew that he did.

He only knew that it felt like a part of him was being wrenched out of place. He was a banker, for heaven's sake. He shouldn't feel a client's pain.

But this was Allie's pain. Allie, a woman he'd known for less than a day. A woman he was holding, with comfort, but something more. He looked down at her and she looked straight back up at him and he knew that now, for this moment, he wasn't her banker.

In a fraction of a moment, things had changed, and he knew what he had to do. He knew for now, for this moment in time, what was inevitable, and she did, too.

He cupped her face in his hand, he tilted her chin—and he stooped to kiss her.

Find out what happens next in
SPARKS FLY WITH THE BILLIONAIRE
by Marion Lennox.
Available April 2, 2013, wherever books are sold!

HARLEQUIN®

Romance

Harlequin® Romance
is moving to larger print!

LARGER PRINT

To provide you with a more comfortable
and enjoyable reading experience, we're
increasing the type size in Harlequin Romance
series print books by about 20 percent.
They're the same feel-good love stories you
want, now easier on your eyes!

Reward yourself with richer romance reading,
beginning April 2013!

HARLEQUIN Romance

"We're going to have twins?"

Kellie Petralia, soon to be ex-wife of Greek billionaire Leandros, is miraculously pregnant! If only their marriage had lasted through the conception.... The pain of being unable to conceive has taken its toll, and even as Kellie surprises Leandros with the exciting news they're just days away from divorce.

But Leandros has other ideas.

Though they might have almost fallen apart, he knows they belong together, and is determined to do whatever it takes to repair their marriage. Will he convince Kellie that miracles can happen more than once in a family?

Along Came Twins...
by Rebecca Winters

Available April 2, 2013, wherever books are sold!